Engaged in Murder

"Romance, great characters, and humor . . . [A] captivating read you can't put down."
—Duffy Brown, national bestselling author of the Consignment Shop Mysteries

"Pepper Pomeroy is a hoot . . . I can't wait until the next book."
—J. J. Cook, national bestselling author of the Sweet Pepper Fire Brigade Mysteries

"[Parra's] protagonist is a bit like Lucille Ball—a screwball—making Parra's mystery light and comedic."
—*Library Journal*

"[A] unique concept . . . Pepper Pomeroy [is] an absolute hoot . . . With a mystery that kept me guessing, Nancy J. Parra has proven that . . . she really is the master of writing the perfect first-in-a-new-series. *Engaged in Murder* pulled me right from the first chapter and I practically read this one in one sitting."
—*Cozy Mystery Book Reviews*

"Parra's latest is a delight . . . [A] quick read filled with relatable, fun characters and a light, breezy writing style . . . Enjoyable and worth reading."
—*RT Book Reviews*

"Definitely a cozy mystery, but with some Hitchcockian overtones . . . with a few thrills and chills thrown in . . . Very satisfying."
—*Fresh Fiction*

continued . . .

Gluten for Punishment

"A mouthwatering debut with a plucky protagonist. Clever, original, and appealing, with gluten-free recipes to die for."
—Carolyn Hart, *New York Times* bestselling author of the Death on Demand Mysteries

"Nancy J. Parra has whipped up a sweet treat that's sure to delight!"
—Peg Cochran, national bestselling author of the Gourmet De-Lite Mysteries

"A delightful heroine, cherry-filled plot twists, and cream-filled pastries. Could murder be any sweeter?"
—Connie Archer, national bestselling author of the Soup Lover's Mysteries

"A lively, sassy heroine and a perceptive and humorous look at small-town Kansas (the Wheat State)!"
—JoAnna Carl, national bestselling author of the Chocoholic Mysteries

"This baker's treat rises to the occasion. Whether you need to eat allergy-free or not, you'll devour every morsel."
—Avery Aames, Agatha Award–winning author of the Cheese Shop Mysteries

"Lively characters enhance Parra's story, and the explosive ending . . . packs a real punch for this cozy. This series promises to be a real treat for readers." —*RT Book Reviews*

"[A] winning recipe for success! As a delicious cozy mystery, it is filled with quirky characters, handsome romantic interests, and at least a baker's dozen of unusual happenings, capped with a twist at the end . . . [A] witty and wily read!"

—*Fresh Fiction*

"An absolute delight . . . *Gluten for Punishment* is a dynamite mystery."

—*Cozy Mystery Book Reviews*

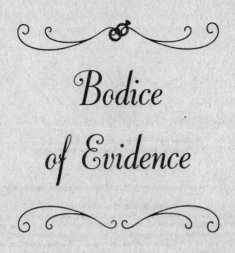

Bodice
of Evidence

NANCY J. PARRA

BERKLEY PRIME CRIME, NEW YORK

BERKLEY
PRIME
CRIME

An imprint of Penguin Random House LLC
375 Hudson Street, New York, New York 10014

BODICE OF EVIDENCE

A Berkley Prime Crime Book / published by arrangement with the author

ISBN: 978-0-425-27036-3

PUBLISHING HISTORY
Berkley Prime Crime mass-market edition / June 2015

PRINTED IN THE UNITED STATES OF AMERICA

10 9 8 7 6 5 4 3 2 1

Cover illustration by Ben Perini.
Cover design by George Long.
Interior text design by Laura K. Corless.

Penguin
Random
House

This book is dedicated to my popcorn sisters,
Terry and Marilyn, fellow sisters in writing
who have been with me from the very early days.
Your love and support have been invaluable.
Thank you for being a part of my life
and my writer's journey.

Acknowledgments

Each book is a team effort and this one is no exception. I'd like to acknowledge a few people who have made this series possible. One of the best parts of this series is working in conjunction with Julie Hyzy, author of the *New York Times* bestselling White House Chef Mysteries. I enjoy bringing her plots to life. Special thanks to my Chicagoland friends who help me keep the details accurate. The book wouldn't be half as good without the support of my family and friends. I don't want to ever forget my wonderful editor, Michelle Vega; my agent, Paige Wheeler; and all the great people at Berkley Prime Crime. You all ROCK.

Chapter 1

♂

Isn't there some kind of unwritten rule that redheads and plaids go hand in hand? I stared at my reflection in the mirror. The green, blue, and yellow plaid, one-shouldered taffeta bridesmaid dress hung on my tall, beanpole-straight body. The picture of the model wearing the gown looked spectacular in comparison to the mirror image of me wearing the giant plaid bow on the single shoulder of the gown. My curly red hair stuck out at odd angles from the static caused by the taffeta.

So much for the understated elegance I imagined a proposal planner was supposed to have. Ever since I'd seen the movie *The Wedding Planner*, I'd imagined that I was a calm, cool, and elegant Jennifer Lopez. The image in the bridal salon mirror told me differently. Sigh.

"I don't understand." My sister, Felicity, the bride-to-be, slumped into the chair next to me in the bridal shop. The pale cream puff of a dress she wore flew up and she batted at the skirt so that she could breathe. "This always looks so easy on those wedding dress reality shows. Oh, Pepper, when am I going to look in the mirror and feel like a bride?" My sister's pretty blue eyes welled with tears. Her golden hair settled about her in perfect disarray.

"This is the fourth bridal shop we've been to," my mother, Abigail Pomeroy, said as she stood in front of us, tapping her toes and crossing her arms. "Didn't you go to that Pinterest thingy online and at least get some idea of what kind of dress you wanted?"

Mom could be a force to be reckoned with. She had created her own small business in our family home. Through grit and determination, she had built her music tutoring venture into a success. It was a tough thing to do in a neighborhood full of cops and firemen. In our Chicago suburb it was a point of pride to be a blue-collar man, like my dad. His plumbing business allowed him to come home for lunch most days. It never ceased to amaze me that my five-foot-two-inch-tall mother could send my father into the bathroom to wash his hands with a single look.

"I did." Felicity's tone was close to a wail. "I've got fifty pins on my perfect wedding gown board." She batted at the café au lait tulle in frustration. "How come when *I* try on the dresses, they don't look a thing like they do on Pinterest?"

"Well, you have to take into account your tiny frame,"

Mom said, and waved her hand as if sweeping from Felicity's head to her toes. "Those models are all around six feet tall. You, my dear, are five foot two. You should listen to the sales consultant. You need less tulle and more drape."

"But I always have to go for less," Felicity complained. "I can't wear bows or ruffles, and now, tulle and crinolines."

"Your great-grandma has a lovely 1920s satin gown you could wear." Mom's eyes narrowed as she started in on the same argument she'd been making for three weeks.

As Felicity's sister and maid of honor, I knew I had to jump in before my mother got any further and Felicity gave up in frustration. Luckily, I had a knack for calming tension in any room.

"Mom." I glanced at my cell phone. "We've been here over an hour. You'd better go check on the parking meter. Remember you asked me to let you know when time got close."

"Oh, right," Mom said, and glanced at her watch. "Your father would kill me if I got another parking fine." She looked at Felicity and held out her hands in a *stop* motion. "Don't move. We'll continue this discussion when I get back." She picked her pocketbook off the tiny couch that sat in the small space of the bridal salon set up for family and friends.

"See you in a couple minutes," Mom said. She scooted out the door as best she could in the three-inch heels she swore she had to wear in case she found the perfect mother-of-the-bride dress. Mom was a little heavy and had a thick waist. She told us to have on shapewear under our clothes so that we would be ready to try on anything that caught our eye. Which was exactly nothing so far during the five-hour marathon of Felicity's dress day appointments.

I bit my lower lip and craned my neck to make sure Mom had left the building. Then I turned to my sister and held out my hand. "Come on. Let's get you out of that disaster."

Felicity took my hand and let me pull her to her feet. The ugly cloud of tulle and lace made me glad I had long arms. The dress took up a good two feet of space in front of my sister. "Thanks," Felicity said as she brushed the wayward material. "If I had to hear her talk about satin and slip dresses one more time, I was going to strangle her with tulle. Trust me, with this much fabric that would have been very easy."

"Turn around," I said. "I'll undo you."

"So sorry I had to take that phone call," the sales girl came rushing into the room. "It was a dress emergency. It seems the bride had spilled pink nail polish all down the front of her dress. Oh, Pepper, you look darling in plaid," she lied smoothly. "Now, how are you doing, Felicity? Is this your dress?"

"No," Felicity said, her shoulders sagging. "The design overwhelms me."

The saleswoman, who was five foot seven and stood only a few inches shorter than me, put her hands on her hips. "I'm sorry, that's the last of our samples and your appointment time is nearly up. Let's get you out of that. Once you're dressed, I'll let you look through my custom lookbooks. Okay?" The saleswoman gathered up the long, beige train and expertly handed it to me. "Hold this and don't let it touch the ground," she stressed. "That's hand-dyed from the house of Asher. We wouldn't want anything to happen to it."

The woman turned on the pointy four-inch heels of her black pumps. She wore a black pencil skirt and a tailored white top. Her brown hair was pulled back into a chic low ponytail. Her makeup was minimal and her fingernails perfectly groomed.

My nails, on the other hand, were a little rough. I tried not to snag them on the hand-dyed train as I followed awkwardly behind my sister. "This was supposed to be fun," Felicity said.

"It is fun." I tried to put on a brave face. "You looked very pretty in all of the gowns."

The saleswoman turned and scowled at me. "Up, up, up!" She gestured with her hands and I lifted the tulle up over my shoulders. She marched us into the large dressing room that was filled with the remains of all the gowns Felicity had gone through.

The woman efficiently unbuttoned the two hundred cream-colored pearl buttons that ran down the back of the designer dress. After what felt like hours, she had all thirty yards of material carefully collected in her arms. "I'll wait for you outside." She bared her teeth in a fake smile and hurried out the door as the sound of the phone ringing in the back room spurred her on.

"Oh, Pepper." Felicity tugged her pale green sheath dress over her head and wiggled it into place. "I am sick to death of people telling me how to dress for my size. I want a dramatic dress. I want to feel like a princess. I don't want to end up with some satin slip because Mom likes minimalism."

"Well, at least she agreed you didn't have to wear Mom's prairie-style dress from the 70's. Although vintage is sort of in. . . ."

"Yes, thank goodness her cousin Herbert spilled wine down the front of it or I'd be hearing nothing but how 70's style is popular again."

Felicity sighed long and hard and I could tell her enthusiasm and mood were failing fast, even with Mom momentarily out of the picture. "You know what? We should take a break and go get some coffee. Let me get out of this dress." I reached under my arm to unzip the side zipper, which was designed to follow a woman's curves. That is if she had any.

"But we have an appointment at Bridal Dreams." She dug inside her navy and burgundy purse for her cell phone. Pulling out the phone and tapping the screen to make it pop up, Felicity finished, "In twenty minutes." She sighed and her shoulders slumped. I swear there was a sheen in her gorgeous blue eyes as she rubbed her forehead.

"Bridal Dreams will wait. You need a break. We would waste the entire appointment if you showed up this tired and defeated." I hung the hideous bridesmaid dress on the padded hanger and pulled on my green sweater and jeans. My mother had been silently disapproving of my shopping outfit. She thought it was far too pedestrian for bridal shopping. I had to admit wearing shapewear under jeans was not my favorite thing to do. Still I only had two types of dresses in my closet—both had been picked out by Bobby, so neither was appropriate for spending a day shopping with my mother.

Dodging any other of mom's comments about my choice of outfits, I had put the emphasis back on Felicity. "After all," I had told my mom this morning. "It's Felicity's day and all eyes will be on her and the gowns she tries on." Mom had frowned but had known I was right. No one even thought about bridesmaids and their dresses until the bridal gown was found.

I slipped on my brown shooties, put my arm through Facility's, and dragged her toward the door. "Let's go get Mom and then grab some coffee and one of those little gourmet pastries with the dark chocolate frosting that you like."

"Oh, no." Felicity shook her head. "I'm a bride. I need to watch what I eat."

"Did you want to look at our custom lookbook?" the saleswoman asked as I dragged my sister to the door.

"Not today," I said breezily. "We're a little worn out."

"Okay," the woman said, with disappointment at the loss of an hour's work in her voice. "Good luck finding what you're looking for."

"Thanks for your help." I waved a short good-bye. We were out the door into the weak sunlight of fall. My sister Felicity had been engaged to her fiancé, Warren, for roughly three months. Unlike me, Felicity had not been planning her wedding day since she had gotten her first princess dress. In a classic twist of fate, my little sister had never spent a thought on her wedding day growing up. Whereas I had started planning the moment my mom had let me tear pictures out of magazines.

Now Felicity was engaged and I had nearly given up on men until Gage asked me to give him a chance. "There's Mom." I steered my sister forward. Two blocks down, Mom was arguing with a meter patrol man. "Oh, boy, let's go rescue her before she drives up the fine or gets arrested."

We hurried down the sidewalk, arm in arm. As we approached, I winced when my mother asked the patrol-man what his mother's name was so she could call her out on the rude way her son acted.

"You saw me come out of Top Brides," Mom argued, her face red with exertion. She flung her arm toward the store. "I was heading straight toward the meter when it ran out of money. I even waved and said, 'Yoo-hoo!' There is no way you didn't hear me. I can be quite loud when necessary."

"Hi, Mom, what's going on?" I asked, and smiled innocently at the young guy in the patrolman's uniform. "I'm sure this nice young man didn't purposely set out to give you a ticket. Isn't that right, Officer?"

His dark brown eyes glittered at me. There was a tight tic in his jaw. "The law clearly says that when a meter is empty and there is a car parked in the slot, then I need to give out a ticket. It doesn't matter if you were sleeping inside the car or coming down the sidewalk, as you suggested. The ticket is in lieu of proper payment." He looked down and scribbled on his pad.

"You are absolutely right, Officer," I said, and put Felicity's arm through Mom's and waved for her to take Mom on down the street. "How much is the ticket?" I asked, and pulled my tan wallet out of my own black leather crossbody bag. "I'll pay it right now."

"You'll have to go down to the county courthouse to make a payment," he said, and barely looked up. "I'm not authorized to take payments."

"Oh, come on, what is it? A twenty-dollar fine?" I riffled through my bills.

"It's a one-hundred-dollar fine." He ripped the ticket off his pad and placed it under the passenger-side wiper blade. "Keep your money," he said as I dug out the bills needed. "I don't take bribes."

"I'm not trying to bribe you," I said, and drew my eyebrows together in confusion. "I want to pay the meter and the ticket."

"Go down to the courthouse," he said as he walked over to his motorcycle. "There's a cashier there." He got on and rode off without a look back.

I took the ticket off the car and stuffed it in my purse along with my wallet. Mom didn't need to see the ticket or know how much it was going to cost.

"I can't believe he gave me a ticket. He saw me coming. The meter had just flipped and he completely ignored my attempts to pay it." Mom's full face was a little pink around the edges and she was hopping mad.

"I'll take care of it," I said, and put my arms through Felicity's and Mom's. "Come on. Let's take a break. There's a sweet little coffee and pie shop three blocks from here." I pulled them in the right direction.

"I can't eat," Felicity said. "And we're going to be late for the appointment at Bridal Dreams."

"You both need a break. In fact, I need a break. Let's go to the coffee shop and concentrate on pie and warm foamy drinks. Things will look better once you've stopped and rested."

"I never thought it would be this hard to find the perfect dress," Felicity said as I pulled them down the street.

"A few minutes and some coffee will help that," I said. "Right, Mom?"

"Yes, that's right," Mom said, and fanned her face. "I do need a break. That ticket got me all worked up."

We walked into the crowded coffee and pie shop. It was teeming with Chicago urbanites. You could tell most of the clientele were local. Their clothes were casual but put together and the women all looked as if they came straight from a salon blowout.

I tugged at my flyaway red hair in a poor attempt to stop the riot of curls. "There's a park across the street. Why don't you two go and find us a seat while I get the beverages."

"Good idea," Mom said, and walked Felicity out the door. "I hate long lines. Ridiculous. They need to hire more people to prevent the lines from being longer than three deep."

Being a small-business owner, Mom had very distinct opinions on how to treat customers. I watched as Felicity and Mom moved across the street. Then I faced forward and shuffled in line. Even though it was autumn, there were so many bodies in the small coffee shop that it was warm enough to need air-conditioning, or at the very least a fan. I perspired as I took tiny steps forward toward the goal of coffee and pastries. I fanned my face and decided it wouldn't hurt anyone if I got three iced coffees and a half-dozen mini blueberry scones.

The scent of fresh-ground coffee and warm berry pie filled the air. People talked, chatting and laughing while we inched closer to the counter. After what might have been a twenty-minute wait in line, I got what I needed. I headed toward the park across the street with a paper cup holder in one hand and a wax paper baggie full of scones in the other.

Mom and Felicity sat talking on a bench next to a small fountain as I crossed the street toward them.

"I know you want the fairy-tale dress," Mom said. "But you really need to be more realistic. Think about the venue and the weather on your date."

"I haven't picked a venue yet." Felicity was near tears. "I know you are supposed to have that first, but it takes so much work to decide on a venue. Is it big enough? Is it inside or outside? If it's outside, what happens if it rains or snows or we have severe weather?"

"What kind of severe weather are you worried about?" I asked as I handed out ice coffees.

"I don't know." Felicity wrapped her hands around the cool cup. "Freak blizzards, the odd hailstorm, or a hurricane. It can all happen."

11

"Then just plan to have an indoor wedding." Mom took a scone with her coffee. "St. Agnes has a nice reception hall."

Felicity actually shuddered at the thought. "No." She was firm. "I don't want streamers and a tile floor. My wedding should be elegant, not like a bad school prom."

"Fine. I have terrible taste. Heaven help the poor girl who gets married in a church like her mother."

"Mom . . ." Felicity said. "You know I appreciate you trying to help."

"Sure you do." Mom took the coffee from me. "That's why you've pooh-poohed all of my suggestions."

"Mom," I said, and opened the wax paper baggie. "Why don't you have a scone? They're blueberry, your favorite."

"I don't need a scone," she said as she reached in and pulled out the top one. "Let Pepper find you the perfect venue if the place where your mother had her wedding reception isn't good enough," Mom said, and saluted me with her drink. "She's your maid of honor. Plus she has an event-planning business."

"Not event planning, Mom," I corrected her, and sat down on the bench next to Felicity. "I plan wedding proposals and engagement parties."

"See, no matter what I say, I'm wrong," she grumbled. "You two realize that I have learned a thing or two in my old age."

"Mom." I patted her knee. "We do appreciate you. But right now this is about Felicity."

"Exactly," Mom said. "There's no reason you can't get your sister the perfect venue for her big day."

"Of course, I could do whatever Felicity wants," I said. "I have connections." Okay, so I had one connection. The brother of the last guy whose proposal I planned had a friend who worked in the Ritz-Carlton hotel in downtown Chicago. Then there was the cousin of the sister of another guy who worked at the Doubletree in Deerfield.

"Oh, would you?" Felicity turned her big blue gaze on me. "I didn't want to ask because proposal planning is your business and I think it's awful to ask someone to do something for you for free when it's their profession. It's like asking a lawyer to look at contracts pro bono."

"Felicity, you're my only sister," I said. "I don't mind helping you. Later tonight we can schedule a time to discuss what kind of venue you're looking for."

"Oh, my gosh, that would be perfect." Felicity seemed to come back to life. "If you're sure."

"I'm sure." I pulled out my cell phone and noted the time. A quick double check told me we were fifteen minutes late to the final appointment. "I'm going to make a quick phone call and let them know we're running a bit late, but we'll be there. I'm certain this happens all the time."

Felicity bit her bottom lip and started to look worried again.

"It's okay," I said. "Seriously, you're the customer and the customer is always right. Besides, they want you in a shopping frame of mind, not a frustrated state of mind."

"Okay," Felicity relaxed.

The phone picked up but went to voice mail. I figured they were on the phone so I left a short message explaining we were on the way. Task done, I hung up the phone. "Okay, how are you feeling? Are you up to making the last dress appointment?"

"Yes." Felicity finished off her coffee and finally smiled. "I'm much better now."

"Good," I said, and stuffed the remaining scones in Mom's big red tote. It was satchel shaped with three zippered pockets to hold just about anything anyone needed to carry, including food, a water bottle, and a selection of first-aid sundries, sunglasses, and an SPF 50 sunscreen. Mom should have been a Boy Scout. She was always prepared as long as someone else carried the tote.

"Let's walk," Mom said. "I've already gotten a ticket and paid for three more hours of parking."

We agreed that the weather was perfect and chatted as we walked the few blocks to the shop. The boutique was a tiny place tucked in between two tall brownstone buildings in an area of Chicago that was in the midst of gentrification. About three quarters of a mile off Michigan Avenue, the shop sat between slummy areas and high-end boutiques.

"Let me go in first and do the talking," I said as I pulled the glass door open and the bells fastened to it announced our arrival.

"Wait, I thought you said it wouldn't matter if I was late," Felicity said with some alarm in her voice.

"You're just fine." Mom patted Felicity's shoulder. "Let your sister do the talking. She's had more practice at arriving late."

Thanks, Mom.

I put on my best event-planner face and stepped into the cool quiet of the salon. If nothing else, I would use my professional calm to soothe any ruffled feathers about our being late. The door slammed behind us as we entered.

"Weird, they must have a window open or something," I muttered, surprised by the wind tunnel effect. "Hello?"

Soft music piped in the space along with the scent of rose and a hint of cinnamon. The waiting room was empty. I went up to the elegant mahogany desk that sat in the far corner. Two gorgeous portraits of brides flanked the wall behind it. A quick peek around the desk told me that the person who usually sat there liked elegant things. The desk had an inkblot pad and sterling silver accessories. A bouquet of fall blooms filled a rose glass vase.

"Hello?" I called again and reached for the silver bell that rested on the desk beside the flowers. I rang the bell. Its tinkling sound echoed through the quiet. "Eva? Hello?"

Eva was the woman we had the appointment with. Most of these salons had two to four consultants working. I figured it must be their break time because the place seemed to be deserted.

"Do you think they gave up and went home?" Felicity asked. She and Mom had taken seats on the twin fainting couches upholstered in pale pink and white stripes.

"Of course not, the door was unlocked and look." Mom turned and pointed at the entrance. "The Open sign is still facing the street."

"The front door slammed. Maybe they're in the back taking a break with the door open and don't realize we're here," I said. "Sit tight. I'll go check it out." I walked down the adjacent hallway. "Hello? Eva? It's the Pomeroy party. We're sorry we're late."

My words echoed strangely down the silk-papered hall walls. There were four doors. The first door on my right was open and showed a large styling room with a three-way mirror, racks for dresses, and carefully placed seats for the bride's entourage. "Hello?"

The room was empty. I walked down to the next door. This one was on the left and closed. I knocked as I reached for the doorknob. "Eva?"

I opened the door and it was a mirror image of the first room. Two sample gowns hung on the rack near the mirror but it too was empty.

Frowning, I continued down the hall. The next room on the right was also empty. "Hello? Anyone? It's Pepper Pomeroy. I'm here with my sister and my mother. We're sorry we're a little late." I frowned when the hall emptied into a final room with some cabinets, a refrigerator, a sink, a microwave, and a table and chair set.

"Where is everyone?"

Startled I jumped and glanced over my shoulder to see that my mother had come down the hall behind me, Felicity behind her. My heart raced and I put my hand on my chest. "Goodness, Mom, you scared me."

"Well, I certainly didn't mean to scare you." Mom put her hands on her hips. "What is going on here? Where is everyone?"

"I hope they didn't leave because we're late." Felicity hugged her pale blue sweater closer around her waist.

"Ridiculous," Mom said with a shake of her head. "What kind of business is this that no one is here and they have customers with appointment times." She went over to the cabinets and opened them.

"What are you looking for?" I asked.

"Evidence," Mom griped.

"What kind of evidence?"

"That they are irresponsible owners."

"Mom, stop," Felicity said, and tugged on Mom's arm. "What if they come back here and find you going through their cabinets?"

"Well, then they'll know they shouldn't abandon the shop, now won't they?"

It was about that time that I noticed the back door was ajar. "Maybe the receptionist has stepped outside for a smoke." I pushed the door open and scanned the back alley for anyone who might look like they worked in a bridal shop. At first glance I didn't see anyone—only a typical big metal Dumpster. "Hello?"

I stepped out to see if maybe they were hiding on the opposite side of the Dumpster. After all, there was a law about smoking within fifteen feet of an entrance. "Eva?"

That's when I saw her.

Felicity screamed behind me.

"Oh, poor thing," Mom said.

An older woman in a white blouse and black skirt—the

17

typical uniform of a bridal shop employee—sat with her back against the side of the Dumpster. She had one shoe on and one shoe off. Her legs were splayed wide. Her head was tilted to one side and the ends of her champagne blond hair swayed in the slight breeze. Her mouth hung open and her lips were tinged blue.

There was a large knife handle sticking out of her chest.

"Call 911," I said, and took a final look up and down the alley, but it was empty. I stepped toward the woman.

"Pepper, don't!" Felicity insisted.

"Don't touch anything," Mom ordered with her cell phone near her ear. "Yes, hello, I need to report a murder. At least I'm pretty sure it's a murder."

I forced myself to pick up the woman's wrist and feel for a pulse. The heat of her skin startled me. Maybe she was still alive, although how I didn't know. Her eyes were vacant. As best I could tell, she didn't have a pulse. I reached into my purse and pulled out a small mirror compact and held the mirror close to her nose and mouth. Nothing.

"She's dead," I said, and sent my mom a troubled look as she relayed the news to the operator.

Felicity stumbled back against the brick wall of the building. Her delicate hands covered her mouth and her eyes were wide. I got up and made a beeline to my sister.

I managed to catch her as she passed out.

Chapter 2

"What happened?" asked a young officer in a blue uniform with the square-shaped chest of a man wearing a bulletproof vest. He had a gun on his hip and a notebook in his hands.

"We had an appointment—" I said.

"There was no one in the shop," Mom interrupted. "Who leaves a store without any employees in this neighborhood? I mean, seriously, who does that?"

"We're going to find out, ma'am," the police officer said. I noticed he had nice strong hands, broad shoulders, and short dark blond hair. He turned his bright blue eyes on me. "When did you arrive?"

"Our appointment was at four, but we were running about fifteen minutes late," I told him.

"So, four fifteen P.M."

"Yes." I nodded. "When we got here, there was no one inside."

"Did you find that odd?"

"Of course, it's odd," Mom interjected again. "What kind of question is that?"

"It's just a question," the officer said, and turned back to me. I admired how calm he was in comparison to my mother, who hugged Felicity and gave him the squint eye. "You arrived at four fifteen for a four o'clock appointment. Then what happened?"

"Mom and Felicity sat down on the couches while I rang the desk bell to let the store owners know we were there."

A commotion from inside the shop caught my attention. A small, thin woman who couldn't have been much older than me pushed through the police. Her brown eyes glittered with concern, and in her hands was a forgotten paper tray with three cups of coffee from the coffee shop. "What is going on? Where's my mom? Why are the police here?"

"There's been an incident," Detective Murphy's voice answered. I turned and spotted my favorite homicide detective coming down the alley toward us.

"An incident?" The girl clutched the tray in front of her. "What kind of incident? I was only gone for a few minutes." We all knew the moment she spotted the feet sticking out from the side of the Dumpster. Her face went as white as a sheet and she dropped the tray. The coffee cups hit the concrete alley, causing the lids to pop off and coffee to splatter everywhere.

I took a quick step back to avoid the splash.

She took off toward the body. "No!"

A policeman stepped between her and the Dumpster.

"No, no, no . . . Mom?" she screamed as he pulled her away.

"Get her inside," Detective Murphy ordered. The young, burly cop nodded and tugged the frantic woman into the building.

An ambulance pulled up to the mouth of the alley. Two medics got out, opened the back of the vehicle, and pulled out a stretcher.

"Pepper." Detective Murphy drew my attention. "Take your family inside."

"Yes, of course." I nodded, comforted by his sincere brown gaze. Detective Murphy was about ten years younger than my father, and he wasn't unattractive. He had that older Humphrey Bogart kind of look. You know, the kind of man that you knew instinctively stood between you and the bad guys. He wore a black, slightly rumpled suit with a blue dress shirt. A navy and white tie finished the look.

I put my hand on Mom's back and walked with her and Felicity into the kitchen area of the shop. The young shop woman sat at the break table; tears flowed from her eyes and her shoulders shook. Someone had gotten her a glass of water, but she ignored it. She covered her face with her hands and sobbed.

"Is she going to be all right?" I asked the policeman who stood beside her with his hand on her shoulder.

"I've called her husband," he said.

"Why don't you move into the fitting room on your right." The uniformed officer we were talking to in the alley ushered us through the kitchen and into a waiting room. "Do you ladies need anything?" he asked.

"Water, please," I said and ensured Felicity and Mom sat down before they fell down.

"No problem," he said and stepped out of the room. The sound of people talking and the general foot traffic a crime scene caused filtered in through the open doorway.

"What time is it?" Mom asked as she patted Felicity's hand. "Your father is going to get worried."

I took my phone out of my purse. "It's five fifteen. Do you want me to call Dad?"

"That might not be a bad idea," Detective Murphy said from the doorway. "You ladies shouldn't be driving home."

"Oh, the car." Mom's eyes grew wide, then narrowed. "I swear, if I get another parking ticket . . ."

"A parking ticket?" Detective Murphy tilted his head slightly.

"Mom got a ticket before we walked over here," I said, and pulled the ticket out of my purse. "I guess that's a good thing now, right?"

Detective Murphy took the paper out of my hand. "Yes, it gives a time and date stamp that proves where you were when the crime was being committed." He looked at the ticket. "Officer Toole will vouch for you. Were you all present when the ticket was written?"

"Yes," we all said at the same time.

"Good," Detective Murphy said, and handed me back the ticket. "Keep that close."

"Your water." The uniformed officer handed glasses to my mother and Felicity.

"Who found the body?" Detective Murphy asked.

"We all did," I said. "I was first out in the alley, but we sort of all saw her at the same time."

"Poor girl," Mom said as she sipped the water. "Who would do such a thing? I mean, this is a bridal salon. Who would want to commit murder at a place like this?"

"That's what we're here to find out," Detective Murphy said. "Pepper, step out with me a moment."

I followed the detective out of the room. The younger uniformed officer stood with my family. He had his hands behind his back and his gun prominent. I knew instantly he was there to reassure my mom and sister that they were safe.

"Tell me what happened," Detective Murphy said. "How did you manage to get involved in yet another murder?"

"Good to see you, too," I said, and tried not to roll my eyes.

"Pepper, this is serious."

"I know it's serious." I paced the hallway. "I'm the one who found her." A shiver ran down my back. "She was still warm when I touched her." I glanced at Detective

Murphy. "That means she hadn't been dead very long. Right?"

"Her core temperature was ninety-seven degrees," Detective Murphy said. "The med tech said she'd been dead less than an hour before we arrived on scene."

"Oh, goodness." I sat down hard on one of the fainting couches in the main room. "We could have been here when the killer stabbed her."

"Try to remember everything you saw."

I shook my head at the thought that my mother or my sister could have been in the path of a murderer. "We were late." I studied his calm, brown hound-dog eyes. "We were supposed to be here at four. We had an appointment, but Felicity was growing distraught at not finding the perfect wedding dress."

"Ah."

"What does that mean?" I asked.

"Ah, as in wedding dress shopping. My sister was ready to stab a fork in her eye before her daughter finally found the perfect wedding dress. They must have looked at hundreds of dresses."

"Well, Felicity is only at seventy-five dresses so far." I hugged myself and rubbed my forearms. "My mom wants to decide for her already."

He sent me a small fleeting smile. "Wait until you go over the guest list."

"I can only imagine," I muttered.

"So, you were late because . . ."

"I talked my sister and my mom into stopping in the

24

park and having a coffee. It was only fifteen minutes. It should not have been a problem."

"Okay, you were late, so you opened the door . . ."

"We opened the door and the front room here was empty."

"Did you hear anything? See anyone?"

"No. Wait. Yes, the door slammed closed behind us. I think I said something about there being a door open somewhere. It's the only way you can get that kind of crazy suction."

"Then what happened?"

"Mom and Felicity sat down here and there." I pointed to the couches. "I walked over to the desk to see if there was a note or something."

"Was there?"

"No, I saw the bell so I rang it. We were pretty noisy. If someone had been in the building, they should not have been surprised by the ringing of the bell."

"Okay." He nodded and wrote something in his book.

"When no one answered the bell, I told Mom and Felicity to stay put while I went to check out the place."

"But you said they were with you when you found the body."

"Yes, they were. It seems that not listening runs in the family." I sent him a weak smile. "Anyway, I went down the hall and opened all the doors to the dressing rooms, but there wasn't anyone in them."

"Do you think that's unusual?"

"I don't know." I shrugged. "We were the last appointment of the day, so I didn't think it was that big of a deal."

"How did you know you were the last appointment?"

"The appointment calendar was open on the desk." I got up and went over to the desk. "See, right here it says 'Pomeroy party, four P.M.' Then nothing until tomorrow."

"The rooms were all empty," Detective Murphy prompted as he nodded at a crime-scene tech to let him know he needed to check out the appointment book.

"When we didn't find anyone, we went to the back room. It looks like a break room and there are bathrooms back there. But the bathroom doors were open."

"What made you think to check out the alley?"

"Well, with the way the front door slammed, I wondered if, maybe since we were late, our salesgirl might have stepped out for a smoke. Then I remembered the state law that people can't smoke within fifteen feet of an entrance. That's when I went around the Dumpster and found her on the ground."

"What happened when you found her?"

"Mom and Felicity saw her at the same time. My sister turned a little green. Thankfully my mom whipped out her cell phone and dialed 911."

"Did you touch anything?"

"Yeah, well, I saw the knife and the blood, but I didn't know for sure she was dead. I bent down and checked for a pulse."

"Did you find one?"

"No." I shook my head and rubbed my arms to ward off the chill that wouldn't leave. "But she was warm. I knew that if she was warm, she might still be breathing. I took out my compact mirror and put it under her nose and mouth. But there wasn't any condensation at all."

"You assumed she was dead."

"Yes." I paced the length of the pink and white front room. "We stayed with the body until the first police officer arrived. I think he introduced himself as Officer Parrack. He also checked for her pulse, but there wasn't any."

"Did you start CPR?"

"Oh," I covered my mouth with my hand. "Should I have? Do you think I could have saved her?" Fear and guilt crept through me. "There was so much blood. I didn't think about CPR."

"There wasn't anything you could have done." A tall, thin man in a black coat marked Med Tech strode out of the hall and into our conversation. He had a black leather bag in his right hand. I assumed it was his CSU kit. "We won't know for sure until the autopsy, but it looks like the knife cut straight through her heart. She bled out." He sent me a sincere look. "Nothing can save a person when they lose that much blood."

"Oh, dear." I sat down hard. The room spun a little.

"I meant to comfort you, not upset you." The man in the med tech coat was beside me in a flash. "Put your head between your knees and breathe in and out."

I did as I was told and things stopped spinning so much. "I know you were trying to help," I muttered to my knees. "But the idea that all that blood could have come from my sister or my mom if we'd gotten here a few minutes earlier is a little hard to take."

"Here." Detective Murphy squatted down beside me and handed me a glass of water. "Sip this."

I sat up slowly and sipped the cool water. "So there's really nothing I could have done?"

"Not a thing," the man said. His gray eyes were solemn. "Now if you don't mind, I need to swab your hands."

"Why?" I glanced at my palms. "You can't be looking for gunshot residue. The murder weapon was a knife."

"It's standard procedure," he said, and opened the kit on the floor next to him. I watched in fascination as he pulled out a tall paper-covered swab, cracked it open, and took my hand in his. "I'm going to hold your hand for just a second."

"Her boyfriend might not like the sight of you down on your knees holding her hand." Detective Murphy winked at me.

"I'm Blaine Wilson, by the way," He introduced himself as he carefully ran the swab over my palms and between my fingers. "CSU."

"Pepper Pomeroy," I said. He took a second swab out of his kit, then gently took the glass of water from me and carefully placed it on a coaster on the white-painted occasional table beside me. He took my hand and turned it palm up and mirrored the swiping he did on my right hand.

"You found the body?" he asked without looking at me.

"Yes."

"I'm sorry for that. She died very quickly. Like I said, there really wasn't anything you could have done." He sat back on his heels, bagged swabs, and marked them with my name, the date, and his initials. "I have a good friend who's a trauma counselor." He reached into his open jacket and pulled a card from his shirt pocket. "Give her a call. These things can sneak up on you. When they do, she's a good one to go to."

"Thanks." I glanced at the card. It said Judith Miller, Trauma and Grief Counselor, and gave a phone number. "I handled the last dead body I found pretty well . . ."

"Keep the card," he said as he stood. "Nice to meet you, Pepper."

"Nice to meet you, Blaine." I shook his hand and he moved off to whatever other duties he had. I turned to Detective Murphy. "Do you know her name?"

"Who? The victim?"

"Yes. I feel like I will carry her with me for the rest of my life. The very least I should do is know her name. Was it Eva?"

He raised an eyebrow questioning my guess.

"Our appointment was with an Eva," I explained.

"Right." He shoved his hands into his pants pockets. "We don't have an official ID yet."

"What about the woman who came back from getting coffee? She obviously works here. It sounded like she recognized her. Didn't she call her Mom?"

"I can't give out the identity of the dead woman until we follow proper channels." He raised his right eyebrow. "You're going to have to wait for the details just like everyone else."

"Of course." I stood. The earth tilted a little as I got that woozy feeling from standing up too quickly. Detective Murphy's hand was out of his pocket like a shot and cupping my elbow. "I'm good," I lied, and stepped away from his touch. "Do you need anything else?"

"I need to get a statement from your mother and your sister. Then you can go."

"Great." I moved to the salon door where my family was stashed. "I'll send Felicity out next."

"Thanks." Murphy sent me a curt nod. "It's best if you don't discuss what happened until we let you go."

"Right," I put my hand on the doorknob. "Thank you, Detective."

"We'll talk again."

"I'm sure we will." I opened the door to see Felicity resting her head on Mom's shoulder. My sister's face was blotchy from crying. "Felicity, Detective Murphy needs to ask you a few questions."

My sister sat up. She pulled a tissue from a paper box, blew her nose, and stood. "That poor woman." She shook her head. "Who does such a thing to another human being?"

"I don't know," I said, and held open the door. "I trust Detective Murphy will find out."

"I certainly hope so." Felicity walked through the doorway and I closed the door behind her.

"What a terrible thing," Mom said, and blew her own nose. My mother's eyes flashed with anger as quickly as they welled up with tears. "No one deserves to die like that."

"The med tech said there was nothing we could have done to save her." I took a seat next to Mom. "Did you call Dad and let him know we were going to be late coming home?"

"Yes, the officer here let me make the phone call as long as I didn't mention details."

"What did Dad say?" I took Mom's hand and her fingers were cold as ice, so I rubbed them between my hands.

"He wanted to come straight down, but I told him we were fine."

"We're all pretty shaken up," I said, and glanced at the officer. "Maybe you should have Dad come down and drive us home."

"What about my car?" Mom asked. "I refuse to get another ticket."

"I can have someone drive the car to your home," the officer said. "Your daughter's right, it would be safer."

"Fine." Mom waved her hand. "Call your father." She sighed and shook her head. "This can't be good for Felicity."

"What can't be good?"

"Murder," Mom said, and turned her wide brown gaze on me. "This is the second murder to get in the way of our planning your sister's happy day."

"I'm sure it doesn't mean anything." I patted her hand. "This has all been so random."

Mom pulled her mouth into a thin line. "These things come in threes, you know. I'm praying that the next one killed is not a member of our family. It can't hurt, right?"

I had to agree. "You're right," I said. "A prayer or two might be fitting right now."

"I'll call the church group and get them praying around the clock that you and your sister don't have to witness another murder ever in your lives."

Now that was a wish I could get behind.

Chapter 3

"I'm glad you called Warren." Mom patted Dad's knee as he drove us home. "Felicity needs her fiancé, just like I need you, dear."

"I'm glad my girls are safe." Dad glanced in the rear-view mirror. "Do they have any idea why that poor woman was killed?"

"No." I leaned forward as far as the seat belt would let me, which was pretty far. Dad had an old Buick with enough space in the back to sleep ten. I kid; it would sleep four. "Detective Murphy said it may have been a robbery gone bad, but at first glance it didn't seem like anything was taken. I do know some of those designer dresses are worth a quarter of a million dollars or more."

"Who spends that much on a dress you wear for a few

hours one day of your life?" Mom shook her head. "Ridiculous. That's a nice down payment on a condo or a town house."

"They are designer dresses with hand-sewn beading and crystals," I said. "You don't expect to be paid 1980s wages. Therefore, you have to be willing to pay today's prices."

"So, wait . . ." Dad made a mad maneuver to pass a slow-moving van. He barely cut back in in time to miss a head-on collision with an oncoming semitruck. The semi honked his horn in anger. "Yeah, yeah, whatever," Dad muttered to the semi. "What was I saying?"

"You said, 'So, wait . . .'" Mom patted Dad's knee as if that would help him remember.

"I forget what I was going to say. What were we talking about?"

"The ridiculous price of dresses," Mom said.

"No, that's not it . . ."

"The murder?" I suggested.

"Close," Dad said, and hit the blinker and pulled out into oncoming traffic.

"Gun it, dear," Mom said absently. "There's another car."

"I see it." Dad squeezed back into his lane just in time to hit his brakes as the traffic in front of us slowed to a crawl. "What was I saying?"

"You said, 'So, wait . . .'" Mom repeated, and I swear I was in the middle of some kind of Abbott and Costello comedy bit.

"I was telling you that as far as Detective Murphy could tell, nothing had been stolen," I said in a desperate attempt to stop yet another *Groundhog Day*–like repeat of the conversation.

"Right," Dad said, and squealed the wheels to take the exit off of I-90 to Arlington Heights Road. "So the woman was killed and the shop left wide open, and as best the cops can tell, nothing was stolen?"

"That's right," I said. "But they need to check with the owner before they know for sure. Turn here, Dad."

"Oh, right, I'm taking you home. For a moment there the car was taking you back with us."

"Maybe you should come spend the night at our house," Mom turned to look at me. "You had quite the scare."

"I'm fine, Mom. Keep going Dad, I'm a half a mile down."

"I know," Dad muttered.

"You shouldn't be alone," Mom insisted.

"Gage is coming by," I said. "I won't be alone."

"How is that going?" Mom asked. "No one thinks it's weird that you broke up with Bobby to start going out with his best friend?"

"Mom." I had to work hard not to roll my eyes. "I told you, I out grew Bobby. I broke up with him before anything happened between Gage and me."

"Not that I was ever his biggest fan, but how does Bobby feel about all that?" Dad asked as he weaved in and out of traffic like an Indy 500 driver.

"It doesn't matter what Bobby feels." I sat back and crossed my arms over my chest like a twelve-year-old. I wondered why being around my parents had us all regressing about fifteen years. "Gage asked me out and I'm willing to see where it goes. I'm taking it slow. I promise. Right now I need to put every waking hour into my new business."

"Tell me exactly what you do again?" Dad asked. Whenever I would start talking about the details of my new business, his eyes would roll back in his head and my words would go in one ear and out the other.

"It's called Perfect Proposals, Dad. I plan proposal events and then the engagement party. Like I did for Felicity. You liked my *Great Gatsby* engagement theme, didn't you? I've got this other guy who wants to do a *Serendipity*-themed proposal. His girlfriend loves the movie."

"See, there's another thing I don't understand," Mom said, her face to Dad as if she knew I would tell her she was old-fashioned and he wouldn't. "What is the big deal about proposals? In our day a guy asked a woman's parents for permission and then got down on one knee and popped the question. There may or may not have been a ring involved. And marriages lasted. Nowadays you kids have to have elaborate proposals, wear quarter-million-dollar dresses, and spend thousands on a wedding so you can spend an equal amount on the divorce six months later."

"Not everyone spends huge sums of money, Mom," I said. "People have budgets they work within. Not everyone is as extravagant as you see on television. And, not everyone gets divorced. There are marriages that last. Probably just as many now as in your day."

"People had more sense in our day," Mom grumbled. "If you ask me, anyway. Not that you did."

"Dad, my place is on the left. On the left!"

He took a left curve into the parking area of my apartment building. Tires squealed and I rolled around the backseat wishing that the big Buick had shoulder seat belts instead of the old-fashioned lap belts.

"There you go." Dad put the car into park and turned back to look at me. "Be careful with that new guy, do you hear me? Lots of people rebound after a long-term relationship. Don't expect too much."

"Yes, Dad, I hear you." I unbuckled and leaned forward to give him a quick kiss on the cheek and then I gave Mom a kiss as well. "Take care of you."

I scooted out of the backseat, opened the car door, and stepped out into the cold and dark. The rear door to the complex was brightly lit so I moved toward it. Dad peeled out behind me. My cell phone rang as I entered the building. I pulled it out of my purse and saw it was Gage. "Hello," I said as I stuck my key in my lock and unlocked the door. "Are you headed over?"

"Nearly there," Gage said. "Are you all right?"

"Yes, I'm fine now." I let the door slam behind me and I tossed my keys in a small basket by the door and slipped my shoes off.

"I heard that you witnessed another murder." There was sincere concern in his voice. The emotion warmed my heart. I couldn't remember the last time a guy sounded like that when he spoke to me.

"I didn't witness it, exactly."

"What does that mean?" Gage asked." 'Exactly'? Are you hurt?"

"No, no, I'm fine . . . really."

"I'm in your parking lot. Hang on. I think this is a story I need to hear in person."

"I'm not dressed for our date," I warned him as I glanced in the mirror above the entry shelf.

"You're always beautiful to me, Pepper."

I couldn't help the smile that lifted the features of my reflection. The sound of the front door buzzer jerked me from my warm and fuzzy thoughts. I pressed the button to let Gage into the building. Then I quickly fluffed my wild-child red hair and bit my bottom lip to bring some color to it. There wasn't any time to fix my face. We might have known each other for ages, but Gage and I had only just started dating.

He knocked at the door and on instinct I peeked through the peephole. Gage was a handsome man. He wore his dark brown hair short and well styled without being fussy. His nose was straight and his jawline chiseled. Gage was one of the few men I knew who didn't have that thirty-something softness in his face. Maybe because he worked out regularly. Something I couldn't seem to find the time to do.

I opened the door. "Hey."

"Hi." His dark blue gaze lit up at the sight of me. It was enough to give a girl a shiver.

"Come on in," I stepped aside and he wiped his shoes on the rough mat outside my door and entered. His hands were in the front pockets of the leather jacket he wore. It wasn't a biker's jacket like my ex-boyfriend Bobby loved to wear. Gage worked a nice Italian leather jacket cut to show off a man's shoulders.

"Wow, you've really done the place up."

I colored at the praise. "I know, right? After I got rid of Bobby's stuff, I realized I didn't have much of my own. I started picking up whatever appealed to me."

"Well, you have good taste." The blue of his eyes darkened and my brain fell out. I stood there like an idiot, staring, until he winked.

"I don't know what's wrong with my manners." I stepped over to the coat closet and opened the door. "Let me take your coat. It's going to be a while before I'm ready to go out." I held out my hand and he shucked the leather coat in one quick movement of his wide shoulders.

Gage was six foot two and toned. He never had any trouble finding a date. Women had a tendency to trip over each other to get to him. It made his attraction to me seem all the more incongruous.

Tonight he wore a barely pink long-sleeved dress shirt, without a tie. It was open at the collar, exposing the strength of his tan neck. I happened to know that he never went near a tanning salon. So how he managed to stay tan in Chicago was beyond me. I could only speculate that he did enough outdoor work that he didn't need to go the artificial route.

The shirt was tucked into dark dress slacks, highlighting his narrow waist.

"Okay, so, you look nice and I'm not even close to ready to go out," I worried out loud as I hung up the coat.

"No problem. After I heard about the murder, I called and changed our reservations to nine."

I caught myself looking at him as if I'd never seen a man before. "You made reservations?"

"Yeah." He shook his head slightly and smiled. "It's what a guy does when he takes a beautiful woman out on a date."

"Huh," was all I could say. Bobby never made reservations. In fact, our last Valentine's Day date had ended up at the bar across the street because even Denny's was packed full.

Gage reached over and lifted my chin with his index finger. "Are you still up for going out?"

"Oh, yeah," I said. "If a man makes reservations, I'm so there." Thankfully I had a little black dress in the back of my closet. I'd bought it for one of Felicity's dinner parties. "Let me pop in the shower."

"A woman says 'let me pop in the shower' and I'm unbuttoning my shirt," he teased and pretended to unbutton the second button on his shirt.

"Oh, no," I said and wagged my finger. "We have reservations." I scooted to the bedroom. "Make yourself at home. There are glasses and a variety of drinks in the antique liquor cabinet." I waved toward the corner of the living area that didn't contain my home office.

"Nice," he said. "Where'd you get the cabinet?"

"It was a flea market find," I said as I rushed into my bedroom. I slipped off my socks and shoes, grabbed clean, date-appropriate underwear, and my brand-new silky robe. "I won't be too long."

"Take your time," his voice trailed behind me. "I like the idea of being here when you get ready for a date."

Wow, why did that sound so darn sexy? When did getting ready for a date become romantic? Bobby and I had dated since my sophomore year in high school. It occurred to me that I had missed out on a lot of things normal women experienced.

I was in and out of the shower in record time. The humidity of the bathroom had my hair curling in mad ringlets. I figured why not go with it. Gage didn't seem to mind that I didn't wear the latest straight style. I had tried it once, but after ninety minutes spent with a straightening iron in my hands, I took one step outside and my hair bounced right back to its frizzy self. I wrapped the robe around me, spritzed curl spray in my hair, and let it do its thing while I applied makeup.

There was a knock at the bathroom door. "Are you decent?"

I laughed. "Now that's the real question, isn't it?" I opened the door and enjoyed the way his pupils widened in his dark blue eyes. Did I mention that he had the longest, thickest black lashes? Something any redhead would give her eyeteeth for. It took me five coats of mascara to achieve his natural look.

"Nice."

"Thanks." I saw that he held two glasses of white wine. "Is one of those for me?"

"Yeah." He passed one my way. "I thought maybe you could use it as you got ready."

"Thanks." I took the glass from his hand and sipped the cold wine. "Okay, I'm closing the door. A girl needs to work her magic far from a man's watchful gaze. It's too early in this relationship for you to know all my secrets."

Gage chuckled as I reluctantly closed the door on him.

Ten minutes later I scooted from the bathroom to the bedroom, threw the dress over my head, put on earrings and a necklace, and tossed back the last of my wine. I walked out in the living room to find Gage staring out the window.

"Hey, I'm ready," I said as I slipped on my shoes.

He put his wineglass down on the coffee table and strode over. "You look beautiful."

Why was it that whenever anyone said that to me I thought they were lying? I swallowed my protest. "Thanks."

I opened the coat closet and pulled out his soft leather coat and my own princess-seamed black wool coat. "What were you looking at?"

He put on his coat and then helped me with mine. "You have a view of The Naked Truth."

"I know." I slipped my hands through the sleeves and then buttoned up my coat. "Kind of weird, right? Bobby picked this apartment."

"I thought you two never lived together." Gage reached the door handle first and opened it for me.

"We didn't. He went with me when I was apartment shopping. When he said this was his favorite of all that we looked at, I signed the lease. A week later I realized the reason he liked it so much was that it was so close to his favorite bar."

"Did you call him on it?" he asked as I locked up and we went out the front door.

"I did. He said that he thought it was a great idea. With the bar so close we'd never have to drink and drive."

"Wow," Gage said flatly, then took my elbow and helped me down the steps and over to his car. "Bobby's a real prince sometimes."

"I know, right?" I lifted a corner of my mouth into a half smile. "I've been here going on five years now. It sort of grows on you."

He opened my door for me. "Will it be hard for you to live so close to the bar now?"

"It's better than living with my mom and dad." I climbed into the car and was happy to see Gage smile when I flashed a little leg getting in. "Don't you agree?"

"Yes." He closed my door for me and went around the back to the driver's side.

The restaurant was an intimate little place that served gourmet local food. I took in the beautiful candles and the cozy atmosphere. "I didn't know you were a foodie."

"Isn't everyone in Chicago a foodie?" Gage asked. "We do have some of the best restaurants in the United States."

"Bobby preferred beer gardens to gourmet. I don't think he even knows what eating local means."

"All you can eat from the grocery store salad bar?" Gage joined in the teasing.

I took his hand. "Let's not talk about Bobby anymore. Okay?"

"Okay," he agreed, his gaze soft. "I've been trying not to pry, but I have to know what happened this afternoon. Can you tell me or is it not dinner conversation?"

"It's definitely not romantic dinner conversation," I said, and placed my free elbow on the table and rested my chin in my hand.

"Then I won't make you talk about it." He squeezed my hand and ran his thumb softly across my knuckles. It was a soothing gesture.

"It's a little awkward, isn't it?" I leaned toward him and asked.

"What?"

"Dating you. I mean that in the best possible way. I'm so used to being around you that I want to tell you everything as if you were still my buddy."

"I am your buddy." He winked at me.

"No," I said low enough for his ears only. "No, I certainly don't think about making out with my buddies."

"And you're thinking about making out with me?"

"Oh, yes," I said. His look had my heart beating fast and my voice sounding breathy.

"Good." He sat back, breaking the sudden tension. "Let's think about that then."

"Okay."

The waiter came over, bringing the bottle of wine Gage had ordered and two wineglasses. The cork was pulled and Gage was asked to inspect it. At his okay, the waiter poured a small amount of the red and offered the glass to Gage. He swirled it like a pro, sniffed it, and then took a small swig.

I watched in fascination as he swished it around in his mouth a moment then swallowed.

"Very good," Gage said.

The waiter nodded and poured a small amount in both glasses. "Enjoy!"

"Really." I leaned in to Gage so that my voice wouldn't carry. "You know about wine tasting?"

He smiled. "You really don't know me as well as you thought you did. Do you?"

"No." I shook my head and picked up my glass. "But I look forward to finding out."

"That's the spirit." Gage lifted his glass. "Here's to us. The most interesting people we know."

I laughed. "Hear, hear." We touched glasses and I enjoyed the wine.

Dinner was a slow, relaxed affair with several courses. It was so strange to have dinner with a man and not have to worry about putting it on my business credit card. It was also different to tell him about my hopes and dreams and listen to his. Time flew by until we were the last people in the restaurant.

Gage paid the bill while I went to the ladies room. The restrooms were well appointed with soft candles and fresh flowers. I made a note. It would be a nice place to contact for Perfect Proposals. I could really see someone proposing here.

Gage drove me home. He parked in the lot and turned to me. "I had a great time."

"Me, too." My heart beat faster and I fidgeted with my purse. "Do you want to come in?"

His eyes glittered in the low light. I felt just a tiny bit daring. I'd never been with any other guy but Bobby, so I didn't know how these things went. Do you wait until the third date? Or was it that you had to know a guy ninety days? Either way, Gage wasn't exactly a stranger.

"I would love to come up, but it's probably best that we wait a little longer."

"Oh." I tried to hide my disappointment but it was tough. "You're right, of course."

"How about I walk you to your door?"

"Okay." I sounded like a pouty child.

Gage chuckled, reached over, and raised my chin with the crook of his index finger. "You are precious, Pepper Pomeroy." He kissed me. It was a long and lingering kiss, and I would have continued it for the next ten years if he hadn't pulled away first.

We looked deeply into each other's eyes. The moment was interrupted by a loud knocking at the window on my side of the car.

Startled, I whirled and bumped my head on the rearview mirror and my left elbow on the stick shift.

"What?"

Bobby's face floated into view as he leaned down to peer in the window. "Pepper, get out here now!"

"What's he doing here?" Gage asked.

"Your guess is as good as mine," I replied.

Bobby banged on the window and tugged on the door handle. "I said, get out here now!"

It would have been easier to stay in the car and let Gage get out and fight with Bobby. But then I was never one to take the easy route. If a situation was going to be uncomfortable, I usually faced it head on. That way there was no blind side. Right?

Chapter 4

"What are you doing here, Bobby?" I asked as I stepped out into the crisp air. Gage came around the car to stand beside me.

"I'm finding my girl out with my supposed best friend." Bobby spit out the sentence as if he could spit fire.

"Dude, you're drunk," Gage said. "You need to take a step back."

"No, you're the one who needs to take a step back." Bobby shoved his finger into Gage's hard chest. "What the hell kind of friend are you anyway? Out with my fiancée."

"We are not engaged," I said. Anger rose up from my toes and burned my throat and cheeks. "You cheated on me for months, heck, years, for all I know. Go home, Bobby. My life is none of your business anymore."

"We've been together since high school, Pepper." Tears welled up in Bobby's eyes. "I got down on one knee."

"I thought we settled this." I sighed at the wreck of a man with whom I had spent so many years of my life.

"Yeah, that's before I saw you with this jerk." Bobby's mood switched back to drunken anger. "How long have you been cheating on me? How could I have not seen this? Best friend, my eye. You've probably been sneaking around on me for years."

Bobby moved until he was chest to chest with Gage and roared into Gage's face. Gage was a good man. He remained calm and stood his ground. The only sign of any emotion was the way he held his hands. If Bobby tried to strike, Gage was ready.

I'd never seen Bobby hit anyone. He wasn't that brave, but then again he was drunk. I stepped in and pushed Bobby back a few steps. "Just because you cheat, doesn't mean everyone does, Bobby." I kept my voice deliberately even. "Where's Cindy? Is she next door waiting for you?"

I pointed across the street. Five years ago all I wanted was to make Bobby happy, and living close to his favorite watering hole was one of many things that Bobby liked about me. I had been so happy he'd wanted me close. What a fool I was.

You know, I always thought of myself as a strong and smart woman. Okay, awkward and uncoordinated also applied to me, but when it came to Bobby, all my smarts had gone out the window. Instead of demanding that he treat me right, I had done everything I could think of to make it work—even spending countless nights at a bar when I hated the whole scene. It was a classic trap, I suppose. One I hoped not to fall into with Gage or any man ever again.

"Bobby, what's going on?" Cindy Anderson approached from the side of the parking lot closest to the bar. She tugged her light jacket close to her neck. Her blond hair lifted and blew in the breeze as if she were a heroine in a movie. Cindy was my polar opposite. She was petite and curvy. Her face was round with high cheekbones and large blue eyes. She wore curve-hugging skinny jeans and six-inch stiletto-heeled leather boots. I couldn't see what top she wore, but it was a safe bet that it was a tight-fitting tee that showed off enough cleavage to attract every man in the bar.

"This so-called best buddy of mine has been screwing around with my girl," Bobby answered her. It was obvious from his expression that he didn't realize who he was talking to.

"What? No, honey." Cindy wrapped her perfectly manicured hands around Bobby's bicep. "I'm not seeing Gage. Are we, Gage?" Confusion showed in her streetlight-illuminated face. "He's dating some other girl. What was her name again, Gage? Samantha or something, right?"

"He was in the car with Pepper." Bobby narrowed his eyes and fisted his hands.

"Well, of course, he was, honey. They're friends. Aren't you, Pepper?"

"Yes," I nodded. "We're friends."

"See? So there's no need to get so upset." She patted his arm. "I've got eyes for no one but you, baby." She kissed his cheek. "Come on, let's go back inside. Tony is running up the pool table and you're next to play."

Just like that, Cindy had his attention, drawing him away from us and back to the bar.

"I'm sorry, baby," Bobby said to Cindy. "I came out for a smoke and got distracted when I saw Gage's car in Pepper's lot."

"It's okay, sweetie," she said as they left the parking area and crossed the road. "I'm here now and I'm not going anywhere."

"Wow," I said as I watched her manipulate Bobby.

"Sorry about that," Gage said, his expression grim. "Let me walk you to your door."

I glanced one last time at the entrance of The Naked Truth. "I think it's time I found a new apartment." I punched in the building key code and Gage held the door open for me. We made our way up three flights of stairs in the four-story walk-up.

"Don't let Bobby make you do anything you're not ready to do," Gage advised. "He's all bluster. I can handle him."

I lifted one side of my mouth in a half smile as I unlocked my apartment door. "Thanks, but I only moved here because that's what Bobby wanted. It's time I found a place where I want to live." I turned to face Gage. He stood just outside the threshold of my door. His handsome face was filled with emotions I couldn't read.

The tension in the silence between us was electrifying. "Are you sure you don't want to come in?"

He reached up and smoothed a wayward lock of hair

behind my ear. "You've had a heck of a day." He leaned in and planted a soft, sweet, closed-mouthed kiss on my lips. "As much as I want to come in, I'm going to stop right here and say good night."

"Oh." My disappointment showed in that single word.

"Your life without Bobby is too new." He straightened. "Let's take this slow. I promise I'm not going anywhere. Okay?"

"Okay." I felt stunned.

"Good night. Pepper." Gage planted another lingering kiss on my mouth. "Call me if Bobby bothers you again."

"Okay." I felt like a parrot but my mind was somewhere around my toes.

He cupped my cheek. "You are a very special person, Pepper Pomeroy. I'll call you tomorrow. Good night." Just like that Gage stepped back, shoved his hands in his coat pockets and walked down the hall to the top of the stairs. He paused but didn't turn around. "Sweet dreams, Pepper."

"Good night, Gage." I said, and closed the door as he headed down the stairs. I locked the door and leaned against it. My mouth tingled and my heart beat fast. I don't know if it was from the encounter with Bobby or the evening with Gage.

I decided to blame it on the evening with Gage.

* * *

The next morning, while I was looking at apartments for rent listed on the Internet, I received a phone call on my Perfect Proposals number.

"Perfect Proposals, this is Pepper Pomeroy, how can I help you?"

"Yes, I'm Alexander Bath. I was at the proposal you put together for Keith Emry. Well done by the way." His voice was gravelly and he sounded like an older gentleman.

"Thank you, Mr. Bath," I said, and grabbed a pen and a pad of paper. "How can I help you today?"

"I would like to hire you to help me propose to my girlfriend. We've been together ten years. I want to make this thing unforgettable. She deserves it for putting up with this old man for so long." He laughed and you could hear the deep rattle of an ex-smoker.

"My fee list will depend on the type of proposal and the necessary planning. Are you looking for something over the top?"

"Exactly," he said. "Over the top. I like that."

"Good, because I specialize in unforgettable, over-the-top proposals. What did you have in mind?"

"I want to propose during a parachute jump."

Okay, that caught my attention. "That certainly is over the top. Tell me why you want to propose while jumping out of a perfectly good airplane?"

That made him chuckle again. "I take it you've never jumped."

"No," I said with a smile and leaned back in my office chair. "I rather like keeping my feet on the ground."

The sun shone into my windows in broad patches that warmed the wood floors and let me see the dust motes dance in the beams.

"You're not much of a risk taker, are you, then?"

I thought of the way I broke up with Bobby and started Perfect Proposals—both gutsy moves for a girl who could just as easily be living with her parents. "I'm getting better at it. Tell me about your girlfriend. Is she an adrenaline junkie?"

"It was actually Dominica who got me into parachute jumping. I'd turned thirty-five. I made a bucket list and parachuting was near the top of the list. Dominica was the jump instructor. She took me tandem with her, and the rest is history."

"Wow, that's a great story." I wrote as fast as I could. "So where is your favorite place to jump? What kinds of things would she like, such as hobbies or mementoes of your life together? Do you intend to propose in midair or just before you take the plunge? I'm thinking just before you take the plunge makes the most sense. Jumping off the plane hand in hand after she says yes and you put on the ring feels very symbolic to me. Wait, no, then your friends and family couldn't see."

"Unless they jumped, too." His voice was filled with laughter. "Yeah, no, that's never going to happen. My mother hates to fly."

"She wouldn't go up for your engagement?"

"No, and worse, she'd kill me if my dad got to see me get engaged and she didn't."

"Hmmm." I tapped my pencil on my lips. "Maybe we could do a helmet camera."

"Let's not put my family or Dominica's in the plane. It would spoil the surprise."

"I can see that." I nodded in agreement. "Let me ask a few more questions."

"Sure, I'm open to brainstorming. You're the expert here."

Alexander let me quiz him for an entire hour as I listed out the must-haves and maybes and "wouldn't it be cool to have . . ." ideas that came to me. I promised him a quote by the end of the day, and if he approved, I'd send him a contract to sign and return with the first third of the price as down payment. Breaking the invoicing into thirds was my father's idea. It ensured the client had skin in the game from the start. The second part of the invoice happened twenty-four hours prior to the proposal event, that way I had at least two-thirds of the money before the event in case the gentleman chickened out or the woman said no and the guy went home disappointed.

The saying *no* possibility was the trickiest part for Perfect Proposals. We hadn't had a woman say *no* yet, but that didn't mean that it couldn't happen. I had to figure in for the risk that the guy would get cold feet and call it off at the last minute, in which case my contract was written so that he owed me 100 percent of the deposits and my billable fees. There was also a full-page addendum detailing what happened if the woman said *no*. All liability was waived at that point. The last thing I needed was for someone to blame the event for the proposal recipient's negative response. My contract lawyer—who was also my uncle, Pete Pomeroy—said it would be too easy to blame me for a *no* when the question was popped.

In fact, he recommended that the couples be screened by a professional counselor before I put down my first deposit on the materials.

At this point in my new business, I did most of that screening by talking to the girl's friends and family, and if I had to, I would come up with a reason to interview the girl herself. I took my cue from those makeover shows, and trusted friends and family to let me in on the girl's life so I could see how she really felt.

Since I was in the business of surprises, it was sometimes hard to find the right balance to get the information I needed without ruining the surprise. If there was any question or doubt on my part, I had the prospective groom spend an hour with my counselor friend, Connie White, for evaluation, and then the prospective bride's best friends were brought in to screen as well. If a woman wasn't all that happy in a relationship, the girlfriends would know before the boyfriend ever found out.

It worked for me, and Connie liked the supplement to her income.

Doing an event like Alexander's proposed jump meant more time at an airport. When my sister's fiancé, Warren Evans, asked me to stage his proposal, it had been at an airport in his private jet. The proposal had gone swimmingly, but the memories weren't all good. I had found my first dead body in the executive airport. After finding the bridal shop salesperson dead yesterday, I was nervous about revisiting any place that reminded me of murder. I mean, what if there was another dead body? Or worse, what if he expected me to jump out of the plane with them?

That made me wonder, would Cesar, my videographer, be willing to jump and record the entire drop? I'd have to call him and see.

I had reached for the phone when I got another call. The caller ID came up with the number of a current client, Mary Ketchum. I picked up on the second ring. "Perfect Proposals, this is Pepper Pomeroy, how can I help you?"

"Hi, Pepper, its Mary, how are you?" She sounded chipper.

I leaned back in my seat and the chair creaked.

"I'm doing well, Mary. What's up?"

"I saw in the paper that you found another body yesterday."

My chair creaked again as I sat up straight and lifted my chin high in the air. "Wait, I'm in the paper?"

"It's in the *Daily Herald*," Mary said. The *Daily Herald* was the daily newspaper for the Chicago Northwest suburbs, and it concentrated on local news. "On page two. They don't list you by name, but they have a shot of the crime scene. You know, one of those vague shots that shows police activity and a general area without showing any details? Anyway, I noticed you in the background. There is only one reason you would be in the shot."

"Maybe because I was in the area?" I suggested. Really, murder did not enhance the proposal event business; quite the opposite, actually. "I was with my sister who was wedding dress shopping."

"Oh, sorry," Mary said, and I heard the crinkle of the newspaper closing. "I thought you should know you were in the paper. I hope it doesn't take away any of your business. Anyway, people who know you know what good work you do."

"Thanks, Mary. I appreciate it," I said sincerely. "How are you? Do you have any more specific ideas for your event?" Mary had contacted me last week. She wanted to show the world that gender roles meant nothing when it came to a marriage proposal. She wanted to ask her boyfriend, Joe, to marry her on video in the hopes that it would go viral.

I worried about going into something with the intention for it to go viral. It was always best to simply record the moment and let it be organic and real. I'd counseled her on that point right from the start. She agreed but had been insistent that I help her plan a big proposal. She wanted to do something crazy cool and just knew in her heart it would get lots of views.

Not that I would mind. A viral video would really help my bottom line. But as far as I could tell, no one really knew how to make something go viral. It either took off or it didn't. I had promised to give her the best proposal she could think of that worked for her and her relationship with Joe, and that was what I was going to do.

"I've been thinking about your advice, you know, going with something that Joe likes and that reflects our relationship."

"Okay."

"We love black-and-white movies. Joe is a huge film buff. Maybe we could do something with that."

"Oh, that's great!" I said. My thoughts grabbed onto the idea and rolled with it. "Do you go to the Music Box Theatre?"

"Yes, it's his favorite special night out."

"Perfect." I whirled my office chair in the sunlight. "I once did a corporate event there, so I know a few people. Do you have a favorite movie?"

"Something romantic?" She sounded unsure. "Or an old spaghetti western." That made us both laugh. "Well, men aren't into romantic movies so much, are they?"

"True," I agreed. "I suppose we could riff off *The Good, the Bad, and the Ugly*." I brainstormed. "It is sort of the theme of life, isn't it?" We both laughed again.

"He would certainly never see a proposal coming," she joined in.

"I'm so glad you have a sense of humor," I said. "Let me work on it. Have you thought about whether you want to get him a ring?"

"I'm still figuring that out. A good friend of mine proposed to his boyfriend and they exchanged watches. But a watch isn't really Joe's thing."

"Does he wear dress shirts and ties for work?"

"Yes, he works for a corporate bank."

"You could get him diamond cuff links or a tie tack."

"Fun idea," she said. "But I don't know. I might just get him a ring. But if I get a ring, what kind of ring do you get a guy when you propose? Boy, this proposal stuff is harder than I thought." She gave a self-deprecating laugh. "No wonder girls let guys do this."

"You're trying too hard," I said. "Stop over-thinking and simply go with your gut. You have good instincts, Mary."

"Okay." She blew out a long breath. "I'll do some snooping in his closet and see what would work best for his wardrobe."

"You can always ask his family," I said. "Part of the proposal event is to have family and friends in on the secret. You may want to start there, especially since you hope this goes viral."

"Right, okay." Mary was quiet for a moment. "I suppose then I need to go see his mother. You know, instead of asking his father for his blessing, I should go ask his mother."

"I bet she would be thrilled."

Mary laughed. "You don't know much about mother-in-laws, do you? Just kidding, Joe's mom is great."

My phone buzzed and I glanced at the call waiting. It was Detective Murphy. "Okay, Mary, I'll get going on the movie theme and get back to you next week. Will that work?"

"Yes, thanks."

I hung up with Mary just in time to pick up the call waiting. "This is Pepper Pomeroy."

"Hello, Pepper."

"Detective Murphy, how are you? I understand you made the *Daily Herald*."

"Not me. They got a nice picture of Officer Flynn. I've

learned to spot a photographer from half a mile away and tend to keep out of their shots."

"Apparently I don't have the same talent," I said as I stood up and stretched. "What can I do for you?"

"I need you to come down to the station and answer some questions."

I frowned and gave a short shake of my head. "Okay, why? I told you everything yesterday."

"It's all part of the investigation," he said. "Can you come down today? Say around two P.M.? Ask for me."

"I suppose."

"Thanks, Pepper. Your cooperation is appreciated." He hung up.

I stared at the phone and frowned. Detective Murphy and I had a bit of a history. He swore he liked me. He said that I reminded him of his daughter, Emily. That said, we had a tendency to butt heads. While he was a slow and methodical pro, I tended to be a quick, hotheaded amateur. Not exactly a good team when it came to solving murders. Wait, solving murders was not what I did for a living.

I shook my head at my thoughts. I was a proposal planner, for goodness sakes—hearts and flowers and romantic fun. That thought made me think of Gage. He was in the prop business for the local theater scene. Plus he was a guy—what a guy. Anyway, he might have some thoughts on what I could do for Mary. I dialed his number without a second thought.

"Hey, Pepper," Gage answered. The sound of his voice

had me all jittery and jumpy. Crazy. I walked to the breakfast bar that separated my kitchen and dining area.

"Hi, Gage, do you have a minute?"

"I always have a minute for you, Pepper."

Okay, now I had to sit down because my knees went weak. I climbed up on the edge of one of my wrought iron barstools.

"What's up?"

"I have this female client who wants to propose to her boyfriend." I ran my hand through my curls and pulled them away from my face.

"That's different."

"Right, that's why she wants to do it. She said he's a movie buff and I was thinking we could do something with the Music Box Theatre. I used to know Sherry Thornton out there. Do you have any connections?"

"Most of the people I know are in the live theater scene in town."

"Oh." I leaned my elbow on the bar and rested my chin in my hand. My little hope bubble burst.

"But I happen to love going to the Music Box Theatre. They played *Moulin Rouge* for New Year's Eve. It was a blast. Do you like independent films? Film shorts? Anything like that?"

"Sure, kinda." I blew out a breath and laughed. "I have no idea. I spent the last ten years doing whatever Bobby wanted, and that meant if I wanted to see a movie, I had to sneak in a matinee before I met him at The Naked Truth."

"Wow."

"Yeah, sad, I know." I sat up straight.

"We can fix that." I could hear the smile in his voice. "We'll make a date to go to the Music Box. They're showing this great Polish film—"

"Maybe we should start with something small," I interrupted, and rubbed my earlobe. "I'm not too certain I'm ready for subtitles." He was quiet and my heart squeezed a little. I vowed not to worry about whether I should have just said yes and pretended to have fun like I did with Bobby. Except I knew where that went. "I want to keep things real, Gage. I really truly don't know and I don't want to pretend that I do."

"That's fair," he said, his tone grew thoughtful and then brightened. "I'll text you the name of my friend who knows someone at the Music Box. That way you'll have another contact in case Sherry no longer works there. Okay?"

"Great." My heart beat strongly in my chest. I had taken a small risk by saying no to his foreign film idea, and he didn't hang up in a silent huff. So far this relationship was doing much better than my last—though that's not saying much. "You are a great friend, Gage."

"I want to be more than a friend, Pepper. I'm willing to take it slow. When you figure out who you are, you'll find me right there beside you."

Wow! Seriously, wow! "Just promise me one thing," I said, as bravely as I could.

"Okay."

"Don't give up on me."

"Trust me, Pepper. I've known you since before Bobby. I'm not going anywhere. That's a promise."

Now that was the best thing any girl, anywhere, could hear from a handsome man.

Chapter 5

"I'm here to see Detective Murphy," I said to the officer at the front desk. The lobby, for lack of a better word, of the police station was a twelve-by-fifteen-foot room with glass windows at the front, uncomfortable plastic chairs against the walls, and what looked like a bulletproof glass sliding door that allowed the front desk to be cut off from the public.

"Your name?" The officer was a wide-faced blond woman with short cropped hair and big blue eyes. She wore a crisp blue uniform with the name Cullen on her badge.

"Pepper Pomeroy," I replied, and flashed her a smile. "He's expecting me."

"Have a seat," she said, and pointed to the plastic chairs. "I'll let him know you're here."

"Thanks," I muttered. On the right side of me were two middle-aged people. The woman sat in the plastic chair and clutched her handbag, while the man paced angrily in front of her. Fall was unpredictable in Chicago, and the temperatures had plummeted to forty degrees. They both wore coats. His was a Chicago Bears jacket. He wore acid-washed jeans and his head was covered by a Cubs baseball hat.

She wore a lightweight navy wool coat that stopped at the hip. Under that was a white turtleneck with tiny red flowers and mom jeans. Her hair was cut in a short shag and dyed blond with lowlights underneath. Her face was thin and pinched, and her eyes were red rimmed.

"I told that kid this would happen," he growled. "I've got a mind to let him sit in there and rot. Might teach him a lesson."

"I don't think that's how it works," the woman said softly.

"How the heck would you know how it works?" he asked her.

I decided I had heard enough of their conversation and moved to the opposite side of the room. There were five chairs lined up by the remaining wall. At one end of the row was a teenage boy with his pants around his thighs. He wore a black T-shirt with a picture of some young singer bent over and sticking her tongue out. He was absorbed in his cell phone.

Sitting down at the opposite end of the row, I dug my own cell phone out and saw that, true to his word, Gage had sent me the name and number of a contact at Music

Box Theatre. Which reminded me, I wanted to contact Jimmy, the gate security guy at the executive airport with a sweet tooth, and ask him whom I should contact to find the best place to produce Alexander's parachute proposal. I was calling it Project Jump.

Looking up from my phone, I noticed a copy of today's *Daily Herald* on the seat next to the kid. "Excuse me, is that yours?" I asked him, pointing to the paper.

He scowled at me for the interruption and shook his head, then went back to his game. I took the paper and found the picture. Mary had been right. I was in the photo just outside the crime-scene tape. The photographer caught me heading back inside the doorway from the alley to the shop. The paper said that the article was on page three.

I flipped the pages to find it. "Woman Found Dead in Alley" was the title of the article. The woman was not yet identified when the paper went to print. At least no one mentioned who had found her. Seriously, I needed to keep my name out of these things. Romance and murder did not mix. It was bad for business.

"Pepper?"

Detective Murphy stuck his head out the door that led to the back. He was a solid figure of a man. Nice looking for a guy who was my dad's age. We might have our differences, but I liked him and, even better, I trusted him.

"I'm here." I stood and folded the paper and tucked it under my arm, before hitching my purse over my shoulder and heading his way.

"Thanks for coming down," he said as he escorted me

down the hall and into the area that opened up into cubicles and rows of desks. The space smelled of old aftershave and even older coffee. Detective Murphy's office was all the way in the back. He had glass walls so that everyone could see into his office and he could see out. Inside was a wide desk and a row of filing cabinets, and across from the desk, two more uncomfortable plastic chairs. "Have a seat."

I sat in the chair closest to the door. His desktop was neat with a black plastic stackable in/out box, a desk calendar, and pictures of his daughter and his wife. He had a big old computer monitor that looked like it was from the 1990s and a keyboard and mouse. "I saw the article in the paper." I put the folded paper down on top of his desk. "Did you identify her? I feel terrible that I didn't even know her name."

"Yes." He said and ran a hand over his face. "Her name is Eva Svetkovska. Is that who your appointment was with?"

"Oh, my goodness, yes. I called and talked to Eva. She was who our appointment was with. Was she a sales girl?"

"No, she was the owner of Bridal Dreams." He leaned forward and put his elbows on his desk. "I'd like to go over the details with you again. You and your mother and sister were at the store because . . ."

"We were out wedding dress shopping for Felicity. She had made appointments at four shops. That one was our last for the day." I clutched my giant handbag. Then realized I must look like the woman in the waiting room, so I relaxed my fingers. I liked leather bags large enough to put my life inside. Felicity liked to tease me that I was like Mary Poppins—anything and everything could come out of my handbag. It didn't help my Mary Poppins image that I disliked jeans and instead preferred to wear black tights, penny loafers, a casual corduroy skirt, and sweater.

"What time was your appointment?"

"It was set for four P.M., but we were late."

"What caused you to be late?" He asked.

"Felicity was having a bridal meltdown and I encouraged her to take a break. We got coffee at the little coffee place about a block and a half from the bridal shop. It made us about fifteen or twenty minutes late. Felicity was worried, but I figured with the price of dresses at the same price point as a new car, the saleswoman would have to be patient."

"And was she?"

"Actually, now that I think about it, Felicity was about to have a second meltdown about being late, so I called and left a message. It sort of pacified my sister."

"I see. Do you know the exact time you got there? It would be helpful."

I pulled out my phone and checked the recent calls lists. "I called at four fifteen P.M."

He took note of the time. "Who did you speak with?"

I frowned. "No one answered, so I left a message."

"Okay, good. I can verify that. How far out were you when you called?"

"Not far. Felicity was a mess, so I checked my phone right before we walked in to show her we weren't that late. I think it was about twenty after four."

"Great." He wrote that down. "Walk me through what happened when you got there."

"Like I told you yesterday, we arrived and no one was there. I rang the bell but no one answered, so I went looking. I thought maybe they just couldn't hear the bell . . . Wait. I remember something else. I may have mentioned it yesterday but it might not mean anything."

"Anything you remember might be a clue."

"Well, when we first walked into the shop, the door slammed behind us, you know, as if there was another door open and the wind sucked it closed. I didn't think much about it at the time, but I don't think it slammed again until the first responders were coming and going through the front and back door at the same time."

"Hmm," he said, and wrote it down next to the timeline I had given him.

"Do you think the back door was open when we came in?"

"Could be." He studied the notes. "Thanks."

"Wait, you don't think it was the killer leaving, do you? We did make a lot of noise when we came in."

"Eva was murdered in the alley," he said, and studied me with seriousness. "Did you see or hear anyone when you entered the shop?"

"Um." I felt a cold sweat wash over me at the idea that the killer was in the shop when we were. "Wow, no. Not that I remember." A tinge of relief followed the fear as I told myself to breathe in and out and think. "In fact, I distinctly remember that the shop had that weirdly empty feeling."

"Weirdly empty?"

"You know, it's a shop so there are usually two or three salespeople and clients inside, talking and laughing or crying or arguing, whatever."

"But you heard none of that."

"No, there was no sound at all. Come to think of it, I remember expecting to hear soft music at the very least and there was nothing . . . except for the door slamming behind us."

"So you are certain no one was in the building except for you and your sister and mother."

"I'm as sure as a person can be." I studied him as I thought. "Yes, I'm positive there was no one else in the shop." I blew out a long breath and relaxed. "You know, for a moment I was afraid we could have been caught up in the crime."

"You and your family were very lucky," he said. "Is there anything else you can remember?"

"Not really. Isn't it odd that no other salespeople were there when we got there?" I pressed. "I mean, a place like that should have a receptionist or something, right? What about the other girl who came in late? Is she okay?"

"I can't share details with you, Pepper, you know that." He sat back. "It's an ongoing investigation."

I bit my bottom lip. "But the woman was so distraught. I heard her call out Mom when she saw us in the alley. Was the victim her mother? Can you at least tell me if she's okay? Is there anything I can do for her?"

"Fine, I can confirm that the victim was her mother."

I gasped and covered my mouth. "How horrible." I couldn't imagine walking in and discovering my mother had been murdered. "But the paper said that the identity of the woman was being held until the family was notified. If the other woman—what was her name?"

"Vidalia."

"If Vidalia was the victim's daughter, why didn't the paper identify her?"

"Vidalia said her mother came over to America from Russia as a teen. Most of her family is still in Russia or scattered around Europe. She asked that she be able to tell her father and the rest of her family before her mother's name is splashed all over the Internet."

"Oh, of course, that makes sense."

"Listen, Pepper, are you absolutely certain you didn't see anyone else at the shop? Would you be comfortable swearing to that in a court of law?"

"Yes, I'm certain there was no one else there. It's why I went outside. It was so strange not to have anyone in an open shop. Especially one where appointments are made. I thought maybe whoever was waiting for us had gone outside for a smoke. It sort of made sense since the door slammed behind us when we went inside." I remembered the scene as clearly as possible. "Wait, that doesn't make any sense."

"What doesn't make sense?"

"If only the victim and her daughter were working, then why did her daughter have three beverages?"

"What? What beverages?"

"When she came through the door, Vidalia was carrying a beverage tray like the ones I saw at the coffee shop. I could have sworn there were three drinks in the paper tray. I mean, why else would you need a tray? Usually if you are carrying two drinks, they don't give you a tray."

"Good point," Detective Murphy said, and made another note. "Was she bringing drinks for your sister?"

"No." I shook my head and drew my eyebrows together. "Unless . . . since there were three of us she might have thought she'd get us coffee if they do that for customers . . . Wait, no, we didn't order anything. How would she know what to bring?"

"Good question," he said. "Anything else come to mind?"

I scrunched my face. "No, that's it."

"Great." He paused and studied me for a moment. "Look, I didn't ask you here only because of the investigation."

"You didn't?"

"No." He stood and shoved his hands in his pockets. "Can I get you some coffee or something?"

I could tell he was feeling awkward and out of his element. "Water would be good, thanks."

"Great, I'll be right back." He practically ran out of the room. His nervousness caught more than my attention. The people sitting near his office asked him how he was and he waved them off. He went around a corner and came back a couple of minutes later with two bottles of water and a paper cup.

"Is everything okay?" I asked as he handed me the cup and a cold bottle of water.

"Yeah." He hitched a hip on the corner of his desk, opened the bottle in his hand, and took a quick swig. "Look, this is weird, I get that, but you know my wife is dead, right?"

I glanced at the photo on his desk. "Yes, I remember. How long has it been?"

"Six years." He took another swig.

"I'm sorry."

"It's okay." He shrugged. "You know, you remind me of my daughter, Emily, right?"

"Yes." I nodded. "You said that." I couldn't help feeling a little relieved that he wasn't going to ask me out. No man asked a woman out after comparing her to his daughter.

"You told me you broke up with that guy—what was his name?"

"Bobby. Yes, we'd been dating since high school, but it wasn't going anywhere so I broke it off."

"How are you doing with that? Are you okay?"

"Is this what this is about?" I shifted. Maybe I had it wrong. Maybe he was going to ask me out. Not that he wasn't a bad-looking guy. There was something appealing in his confidence and bad-guy-fighting demeanor.

"It's about my daughter, Emily." He got up and paced. "I need some advice."

"Oh, sure." I let out a breath I didn't know I was holding.

"She's a nurse anesthetist, lives in California—too darn far away if you ask me."

"She sounds smart and successful," I said as encouragingly as I could.

"Exactly," he said, and turned to me. "But she's living with this loser who treats her bad. When you told me about your guy . . . what was his name?"

"Bobby."

"Yes, Bobby," he said. "When I told you that you reminded me of Emily, it was especially true when you talked about that guy."

"Oh, dear."

He sat back down on the edge of his desk and leaned toward me. "What I want to know is how to encourage her to stand up for herself and do what you did."

"You want her to break up with him?"

"Yes, she deserves better. The guy hasn't had a job in two years. All he does is lie around her apartment playing video games. It's ridiculous." He crossed his arms. "I tried to tell her, but she refuses to listen. So I thought—"

"You thought maybe I could help you," I finished.

"Yeah." His shoulders slumped. "Was there anything your parents did that helped you to see the light where that Bobby guy was concerned?"

"No," I said, then shook my head and sent him a wry smile. "My parents loved Bobby."

"Seriously?" He looked aghast.

"That's what I thought, anyway," I said as I fiddled with my purse. "Until I broke up with him. Then they told me what they really thought."

"They hated him."

"Let's just say they thought I could do better. When I asked them why they didn't say anything, my mom said it was because they trusted me to figure things out on my own."

"Oh." His expression fell.

"Listen, maybe this guy isn't so bad. I'd be happy to give you some perspective. What don't you like about him, besides the job thing? It's a tough job market out there. I should know. I was downsized recently myself."

"But you've started your own business," he pointed out. "As far as I can tell, this guy doesn't even attempt to look for a job. The kid is supposed to be an IT expert. I gave him the business card of a buddy of mine who runs a security firm out there. He never called him."

"Yeah, that sounds bad. What did your daughter say about it?"

He shoved his hands in his pockets. "She defends the guy. She says he doesn't do security IT. I told her that Martin could connect him to others in the community, but she said her guy was fine. He had some huge severance package that he was living off of and he didn't need my connections. Plus he has some buddies in the business, so that was the end of that."

"When was that?"

"A year and a half ago," he grumbled. "I don't get it. If he had connections, why not get a new job and have both the severance and the new job?"

"So the lack of a job is the biggest thing bothering you about him?"

"There's more to it." He shrugged and moved back to his chair. "Let's call it a cop's gut instinct." He sat down. "You figured things out about that Bobby guy on your own, right?"

I smiled softly. "Yes, but I wish I had done it sooner."

"But your folks didn't tell you . . ."

"No." I shook my head. "They knew it would make me want to stay with him longer. It's a kid thing . . . No, it's more than that. I have girlfriends who hate it when you tell them their guy isn't good enough for them. It's sort of insulting, you know?"

"Right."

I stood. "She sounds like a smart girl. You raised her well. Be patient with her. If her boyfriend is as bad as Bobby, she'll leave him on her own."

"You're probably right," he said. "Thanks for the talk."

"Hey, no problem. We're friends, right?"

"Yes. Like I said, you remind me of her. Stay out of trouble, okay?"

"Okay," I said. My phone rang as I walked out of the police station. It was my sister, Felicity. "Hello?"

"Vidalia from Bridal Dreams called," Felicity sounded out of breath. "She apologized for no one being in the shop when we got there yesterday. Pepper, she wants me to reschedule my dress appointment. That's weird, don't you think? I mean, weddings and murders don't really go together."

"Yes, that is odd," I agreed and left the building so that

no one could overhear me. "Especially since Detective Murphy told me that it was her mother, Eva, who was murdered in the alley."

"Yikes. So no, I'd rather go back to one of the other shops and get my dress."

"Wait," I said. "Make the appointment."

"Why?" Felicity sounded horrified.

"I want to ask her some questions."

"Pepper, you don't have to investigate this."

"I know that, but I'm the one who found her mother. I feel responsible."

"Pepper—"

"It's only a few questions. Think about it. If Mom were murdered, wouldn't you want someone to care enough to help find her killer? Besides, this murder must be hurting her business. I know what that feels like. Can you imagine losing your mother and your income? We should go and show our support."

"Fine, but I'm not buying a dress there."

"I'm not saying you should," I agreed. "I'm free this evening or tomorrow morning. Whichever works out for you."

"Pepper, give her some time. I'm sure she has a funeral to attend to and all kinds of other details."

"Then next week, whatever, as long as it's soon. It is easier to solve a murder in the first forty-eight hours, or so I've heard."

"You watch too much television," Felicity accused. "I am not making the appointment in the first forty-eight hours. It's too creepy."

"Okay, but don't wait too long."

Felicity sighed loudly. "Fine, I'll call her back and let you know when the appointment is, but I'm not dragging Mom into this. She's had enough of a shock for one week."

"Thanks, Felicity. I love you."

"You remember this when I make you wear the plaid bridesmaid dress," she threatened.

I laughed as I hung up. I knew better. My sister wouldn't want anyone to look bad in the pictures of her big day. Not even her nosy sister.

Chapter 6

The first forty-eight hours came and went without even
a peep from Detective Murphy. I was busy with Mary's
movie-themed engagement and Alexander's Big Leap—
which sounded much better than Big Jump or Big Plunge.

I was in Mom's kitchen snatching veggies off the appe-
tizer platter while she put the finishing touches on dinner.
Mom and Felicity and I were supposed to powwow about
wedding plans, and I never turned down a free dinner.

"Gage's contact at the Music Box Theatre was a dream,"
I said, and chewed on a carrot dipped in ranch sauce. "He
loved the idea that the proposal could go viral and promote
the theatre."

"The Music Box Theatre, that's the one that does all
the film festivals and independent movies and such, right?"

"Yes." I was impressed. "I had no idea you knew about the Music Box."

"I read the theater section of the *Tribune*," Mom said.

"What's going on?" Felicity asked as she came in the back door. She wiped her feet and took off her fall jacket and hung it on a peg next to the door.

"Mom's a hipster," I teased, and snagged a piece of celery.

Mom frowned and pulled the tray out of my reach.

"I knew that," Felicity said, and patted Mom on the back as she took a carrot off the tray. Mom sighed and ignored the infraction.

I made a face at my sister and whispered, "Suck up."

"Dinner's ready," Mom called to Dad as she put the veggie tray on the dining room table. "Go wash up."

We all trudged off to wash our hands. I glanced to make sure that Mom wasn't behind us, then whispered to my sister, "Did you make the dress appointment?"

Felicity soaped up her hands. "Yes, and it was hard. The woman practically begged me to come back in and give her a chance." She ran water over her hands as I soaped mine. "She apologized again and said that she was only out for a short break when we got there. She'd walked down the block to that coffee place we were at, remember?"

"Sure," I said, and ran water over my hands as Felicity dried hers. "Strange, I don't remember seeing her."

"We wouldn't remember if we had. We hadn't ever met her before, silly. Anyway, she said she chitchatted with the baristas for a while, had a cup of coffee at a table by herself, and then bought more, for herself and her mother."

"That explains two of the coffee cups in her carrier," I said as I towel dried my hands. "But who buys coffee to go after you had a cup in the café? And what about that third cup I saw?"

"I don't know, I didn't ask. She sounded so distressed on the phone. She kept saying she knew that they had a four o'clock appointment, but her mom said that she'd handle it alone. So, she didn't hurry."

"Who didn't hurry?" Dad asked as he stepped in the bathroom to wash up.

"No one," I said at the same time that Felicity answered.

"This girl who missed our dress appointment."

"Which is it?" Dad asked. "No one or a shop girl?" He gave me a serious glare under his white brows.

"The shop girl," I admitted, and slinked out of the bathroom.

Dad harrumphed and turned on the water. I pushed my sister out into the kitchen. "When's the appointment?"

"Friday at one."

"Good, I'll be there."

"Be where?" Mom asked. I jumped at the sound of her voice. How did she get behind me?

"At the dress appointment the shop girl wasn't on time for last week, I'm guessing." Dad kissed Mom's cheek. "Let's eat. You girls get started talking wedding out here and my dinner will get cold."

"Well, we certainly can't have that," Mom said, and urged us all into the dining room.

I gave Felicity the eye. She shrugged as if to say, *What is done is done.*

Maybe not. Maybe I could distract Mom.

After we said grace and Dad got his meat and potatoes, I filled a third of my plate with salad and passed the bowl to my sister. "I have this client, Alexander, who wants to propose to his girlfriend on a parachute jump."

"That's unusual," Mom said politely as she filled her plate with two vegetable servings, one protein and one starch. It was the diet she had learned in high school, and to this day she swore by it.

"Who would want to jump out of a perfectly good airplane?" Dad asked.

"Apparently Alexander's girlfriend, but it's not the jump that's the issue. It's what to do with the family and friends."

"Oh, I certainly hope he doesn't expect everyone to jump out of a plane," Mom said, her fork frozen halfway to her roast beef.

"No, I got him to agree that that was a bad idea. The problem is that he still wants them all involved. But if they all go up in the plane, it looks suspicious and will ruin the surprise. But if he asks in midair, then no one will be there to witness."

"You could have him wear one of those helmet cams," Felicity said as she downed her green beans.

"I tossed around that idea," I said. "I could stream it to a television screen for the family to watch live."

"That's all nice and good," Dad said as he took a second helping of roast beef. "But that's not exactly being involved."

I scrunched up my face and sighed. "No, it's not."

"What if you have the family gather at the landing site and hold up cards—you know like the ones they use to spell stuff out at football games?" Felicity asked.

"Oh, that's good," I said. "They could all be on the ground with a card for her name and then a card for 'Will you' and one for 'marry me?' Both Alexander and his lady love would be wearing helmet cams so we get both points of view—hers when she sees the signage and his when he gets the answer. They can touch, hold hands, and then float to earth where, surrounded by family and friends, he can present the ring."

"Oh, that sounds perfect!" Felicity clapped.

"It is rather romantic in a group sort of way," Mom said. "Much better than him trying to slip a ring on her hand several thousand feet in the air. Can you imagine what would happen if he dropped it?"

"Oh, no." Felicity's eyes went wide. "They'd never find it."

"Someone else would get hit in the head with it and would either feel cursed or blessed," Dad said. "Probably cursed. A rock hurtled at your head' s gotta hurt, no matter how small."

"Dad!"

"Frank!"

"Daddy!"

We all chided him at the same time and he grinned. "Well, it would. Diamonds are the world's hardest rocks."

"Not if it hit your stubborn old head," Mom muttered. Felicity and I giggled. Dad winked. "It isn't going to happen. Pepper will have the event well in hand."

"Maybe I'll suggest that his best man hold the ring until they land and he goes down on one knee," I said.

"Good idea," Felicity said.

"Good, now that that is discussed, when is the dress appointment?" Mom asked.

I bit my lip and quickly stuffed my mouth with salad so I wouldn't have to say anything.

"What dress appointment?" Felicity tried to give Mom the innocently blinky look, but Mom was too much on the ball to fall for that.

"The one you girls were talking about in the bathroom without me."

"Were we talking about a dress appointment?" Felicity asked me.

I shrugged and continued to chew.

"You were," Dad said, and eyed Felicity over his water glass.

"Oh, that appointment," she said with a guilty flush.

"Yes, that appointment," Mom said, and broke a rule by crossing her arms on the table. "When and where is it, and why don't you want me to go?"

"I haven't decided if I'm going," Felicity said, and sipped her water.

"Why not?" Mom drew her dark brows together. "Pepper?"

"Don't ask me," I said, and forked up more salad. "I want to go to the appointment."

"Felicity?"

"It's the daughter of the woman we found murdered in the alley. She wants us to come back. She told me her mother started the business and she wants to continue with it in her mother's memory."

"Oh, that's sweet. You should go."

"Mom, no. I don't want my wedding associated with a murder. It was bad enough that my engagement was. It was unbearable when Warren was arrested. I don't want that memory."

"I understand, dear," Mom said, and patted Felicity's hand. "But you might be able to get a really good deal."

Leave it to my mom to equate murder and misfortune with a sale. I bit back a sigh.

"Never hurts to look," Dad said, and dug into his beef. "You haven't found the dress you want yet, right?"

I wasn't surprised when Dad sided with Mom. They were paying for the dress. The thought made me smile.

"What?" Felicity asked me. "I already know why you want me to go."

"Why do you want her to go?" Mom asked.

"She wants to question Vidalia and see if she can help Detective Murphy solve another murder." Felicity made a face at me.

"Is that true?" Mom asked.

"It's a great excuse," I said, and shrugged. "It seems weird that she went to a coffee shop, sat alone for a while, drank coffee, and then came back with three cups—just in time for the police to find her mother dead in the alley."

"Oh, dear, you think she did it!" Felicity wailed. "Now I can't go in there. If I buy my dress from a killer, it has to be bad luck."

"No, no." I patted my sister's hand. "I don't think she did it. If she did, she wouldn't be begging for us to come back, would she?

That gave Felicity pause. "No, I guess not."

"See, it'll be all right." I put my arm around her shoulder and gave her a hug. "I only want to find out why she had three cups of coffee. Maybe someone else was supposed to be there. Someone that may know more about what happened to her mother."

"That does make sense," Mom said. "Come on, keep the appointment. We'll all go."

"Are you sure you want to go back to the scene of the crime?" Felicity asked Mom. "I don't want you to get another bad shock. It can't be good for you."

Mom laughed loudly. "I might be old, but I'm not that old," she said. "I promise I'm not hiding any heart problems. I just saw Doctor Eckhart. I'm fit as a fiddle for a woman my age. I'm sure I can handle a dress shop."

"If you're sure," Felicity said.

"I'm sure," Mom said. "And I promise, I won't ask you to buy a dress—no matter how deeply discounted. Unless you love it and it's the perfect dress. Isn't that right, Frank?"

"Right," Dad said. "What's for dessert?"

"It's crème brûlée, and you can wait," Mom chided him and reached over and patted his tummy before turning back to Felicity. "So, it's settled. You'll keep the appointment and we'll all go. It may help the poor girl feel as if she is moving forward in her life, and perhaps Pepper can discover something to help Detective Murphy."

"Fine, but if I feel the least bit weird about the dress, I'm taking it off and leaving. Is that clear?"

"Perfectly," Mom and I said in unison.

"Good, now that's settled. Let's bring on the dessert." Dad grinned and I had the feeling Felicity's dress shopping was going to get a whole lot more interesting.

Chapter 7

♂

"Welcome, I'm Vidalia," the young woman said as she greeted us at the door. "I'm so glad you came. Please come in. Can I get you some sparkling water?"

"Yes, please," Mom said behind us. "It's good to stay hydrated. Dress shopping can get quite involved."

"I see you've been wedding dress shopping before," Vidalia said over her shoulder, and walked us into the first salon. "Please have a seat and make yourself comfortable. My time is entirely yours. My mother's case is still open with no leads, but now that the funeral is over, I'm so glad to be back to work. Thank you again for coming in. You are the first group to return. I'm hoping others will see that I'm still in business and have my mother's uncanny knack to place the right dress with the right bride. Trust me. I can get you in the dress of your dreams in three try-ons."

"Good luck with that," I said. "We've already gone to four shops and tried on far more than three dresses."

Felicity sighed long and loud. "It's not my fault. None of the dresses look like the pictures when I try them on."

"Of course they don't," Vidalia said, and patted Felicity's hand. "The models are all six feet tall with no curves. I promise I have an eye for the perfect dress for real women. Now, there are petit fours on the side table along with a fruit plate. Help yourself." She held up her hand. "Don't tell me you are dieting for the wedding. That's foolish. Your fiancé wants to marry the woman he got engaged to, and I know how to make you look like the bride of both your dreams. I'll be right back with the drinks and the dresses."

"Dresses? But I haven't told you my size yet."

She smiled a secret smile. "I'm guessing a size four, right? You have just the right amount of curves." Vidalia tilted her head and pursed her lips. "You do have a tiny waist, but we can tailor it."

With that she walked out, closing the door behind us.

"Well, she certainly is interesting," Mom said, and took off her jacket and hung it on the ornate coatrack near the table of goodies.

"I don't know how she can claim to find the right dress so quickly." Felicity crossed her arms and pouted. "You know how hard we've looked."

"What are you going to do if she finds it?" I asked,

and picked up a small white plate from the stack on the table and popped some grapes and a couple of the little iced cakes on it.

"We'll cross that bridge when we come to it," Mom said. "We all know how Felicity feels about buying her dress here. We're only here out of respect for the poor girl. It would be horrible to lose your mother and your business in one fell swoop."

Felicity paced. "How did she know my size? I know I'm petite. Usually people assume I'm a size two but she guessed correctly that I'm a size four on top."

"She's a dressmaker and she most likely has a dress-maker's eye," Mom said. "Isn't it wonderful that she can simply look at you and assess your size?" "

"No," Felicity pouted. "Now I'm feeling fat because she didn't assume I was a size two."

"Oh, stop," I said, and sat down. "You are far from fat. Besides Warren loves you exactly the way you are. "

"You only say that because you are tall and thin." Felicity crinkled her nose at me. "At least I have boobs."

"Girls!" Mom said. "Enough. Felicity, if you don't like it here, we can leave."

"But—" I said.

"No *buts*." Mom held out her hand to cut me off. "This is about Felicity, not your questions. Do you understand?"

"Yes, ma'am." I slumped into the couch. "Sorry, Felicity. I promise we can leave anytime you want."

The door opened then and Vidalia came in with three dresses draped over her arm. Behind her was another woman who appeared to be in her twenties. She had a short brown pixie cut, dark winged eyebrows with a diamond stud in the corner of her right eyebrow, and a sweet smile. She wore a black shift dress that matched Vidalia's, and bright red lipstick.

"This is my assistant, Theresa," Vidalia said. "She has your waters and can get you anything else you need."

Theresa carried a pretty lined wicker basket filled with ice that held three bottles of water. "Hello, it's so nice to meet you. I want to apologize for no one being here the day of your original appointment. I was out sick, but I'm much better now." She handed Mom the basket. "Please let me know if you need anything at all. I'll be outside at the front desk."

As Theresa left, Vidalia turned to the wall where there were three dress hooks. "I'll hang these up. Now, don't look at them on the hanger," she warned. "This is not about what they look like when they are hanging. This is about how they look on your body."

"Wait, one is pink," Felicity said, "And one is pale blue."

"Pastel dresses are the latest thing," Vidalia said. "Trust me. Many brides are tired of dressing like a marshmallow. Besides, in some countries white is actually a funeral color. That said, if you like the gown but not the color we can order it in white. Okay? Now, remember these are sample sizes and your gown will be custom-made for you here at Bridal Dreams. You can change behind the screen. I have hung up a silk slip that will help the dresses float over your body and keep the lace from scratching."

Vidalia and Felicity stepped behind a three-panel screen with a gorgeous Japanese mountain scene painted on the front.

The rest of the room had pale peach painted walls and soft blue lighting. The corner across from the screen held a dais surrounded by three full-size mirrors. We were seated in two of three peach-and-white-patterned chairs with heart-shaped backs. Mom's had alternating peach and white stripes. Mine had a checkered pattern, and the final one was upholstered in peach fabric with tiny white roses on it.

"The dress she took in looks like a pink cupcake," I whispered to Mom.

"I'm not certain how I feel about colored dresses," Mom said quietly to me. "You father is a traditional man."

I had a feeling Dad wasn't the one who would mind, but I simply stuffed a chocolate petit four into my mouth. On the final wall was an ornate buffet made of oak with the platters of goodies on top. Mom had put the basket on the floor between us, then bent down and picked up two bottles and handed me one. I opened it up to the sound of fizz. Looking at the label, I realized this was the good stuff. No cheap bottled water here.

"How's it going back there?" Mom called.

"The dress fits like a glove." Felicity's voice floated over the top of the screen.

"Except the waist." Vidalia's voice followed Felicity's. "I'm doing a little pinning so that you get the proper effect."

In a minute Felicity stepped around the screen. She looked gorgeous in the pale pink tea-length gown with lace and a tulle princess skirt and a sweetheart neckline.

"Oh," Mom said, and tilted her head to study Felicity as she walked to the mirrors and stood on the dais.

Vidalia adjusted the skirt and waited a moment before asking. "What do you think?"

"It's very pretty," Felicity said.

"It makes you look like a princess," I encouraged.

"What do you like about it?" Vidalia asked my sister.

"You know, I kind of like the lace. It's got a full skirt that isn't so full that I have to move sideways through the doors."

"And that's important," Mom said. "She has to be able to walk down the aisle with her father."

We all giggled at the idea of the dress walking down the aisle first, then Felicity, then Dad. "It sort of looks more like a prom dress than a bridal gown, but it's beautiful," I said, and popped a grape into my mouth. I had sworn never to say anything negative about any dress my sister tried on. I was not going to be the one to ruin her perfect gown.

"Remember, this is the first of three," Vidalia said. "Mother taught me that you should show the bride options so that she can understand why you picked the dress you picked. This color is new and fresh and makes your skin look lovely."

"I do like it," Felicity said, as she twisted and turned in the mirror, eyeing all angles. "But I don't love it."

"Let's get you out of it and then I want you to take a moment and have some water and relax. It's important that you don't rush from dress to dress. Okay?"

"Okay," Felicity said.

"Good." Vidalia followed her back to the screen.

I got up and followed them, leaning against the wall. It was time to start asking questions. "How are you doing, Vidalia? This has to be difficult—working without your mother here."

"Truthfully, I'd much rather be working. I'm so glad you and your family came back. It really helps me."

"This choice of dress was unique and lovely," I said.

"Most brides come in here looking for a strapless mermaid dress, but I believe that each bride needs to wear the dress created for her body and her personality. Not simply a sexy white gown." She tugged the tulle and lace over Felicity's head. My sister's blond hair floated back down and rested perfectly around her shoulders. She wore a silk slip that did indeed skim her figure.

"Wow, that slip would make a nice dress," I said.

"I was afraid mom would have the same thought." Felicity winked at me recalling our mother's preference of satin slip dresses.

"I did have that thought," Mom said with a pout. "But I bit my tongue. You two have made it quite clear that a slip dress is not for you."

Vidalia hung the pink dress back on its hanger and

fluffed all the little bits of lace and tulle back into place. "Your mother is right. A slip dress would be perfect for a bride of your height and weight," Vidalia said, "but I'm thinking that you really want something more elegant and refined. Am I right?"

Felicity's eyes grew wide. "Yes," she said. "How did you know?"

"Oh, my goodness, it's simple, really. I can see your style in the cut of your hair, the clothes that you wore into the salon, and the type of diamond on your finger." She pointed to the princess-cut rock on Felicity's left hand. "I'll take this out and hang it up. Please take a moment to get some water and have some fruit."

She walked out with the gown and closed the door behind her.

"I kind of liked the pink," I said, feeling guilty for my earlier comment on the prom dress.

"How did she know I was thinking about a strapless gown with a mermaid skirt?" Felicity asked as she opened the bottle of sparkling water and sat on the chair beside Mom. "Did you notice how she made it sound as if everyone wanted that type of dress, but she knew it was not for me?"

"She's very clever," I agreed, and wandered toward the two dresses that were left. They were safely tucked into clear dress bags, so it was difficult to tell anything about their true shape.

"Hi, Vidalia must take a phone call and sent me in to check on you." Theresa entered the room with a tray. "I thought I'd bring in some coffee. There's this great café down the road and so I ran out and got you all some caramel lattes. Please do take special care to keep the coffee away from the dresses. We don't want any spills or stains. But since you are waiting for the fitting, I'm certain it will be fine."

"Oh, how sweet of you," Mom said.

I wasn't so convinced. "You left the front desk to get us coffees? What if you had other customers come in?"

Theresa blushed. "Oh, well, we don't have anyone else scheduled, so I thought I'd make a quick run."

"It was very nice of her," Mom said slowly, as if I were being ridiculous.

"Yes, sure, it was nice," I said, and crossed my arms. "You said you were sick the day that Eva was murdered?"

"Yes," she said as she put the coffees on the buffet and straightened the tea plates and silver on the table. "Is there anything else I can get you? More water? More petit fours?"

"We're good," I said as I watched her hover. "Did Detective Murphy interview you?"

"Yes." She turned to me and raised her pierced brow. "Why? I really was sick. You can ask my mother."

"You still live with your mother?" Felicity asked.

"Yes, the economy is terrible. Mom needed help with the mortgage, so I pay rent and we became, like, roommates." She clasped her hands together.

"Oh, what a nice solution. I have a friend who bought a house with her daughter, that way neither of them had to pay a full mortgage," my mom chimed in.

"It must have been a shock when you saw the news," I said, noting how her hands fluttered to her neck and then cheek before she drew them behind her back. It was pretty clear to me that the subject was unnerving for her. Was it because she was guilty of something, or was she thinking about how she could have been here when the murder happened?

"It was terrible." She shifted again, hugging her waist. "I keep thinking about poor Eva in that alley all alone. I can't decide if I'm upset because I wasn't here or stuck on the possibility that if I had been here, I might also be dead, you know? These things can make a person think . . ." Her voice trailed off. Then she brightened. "Perhaps that isn't a good subject for today. After all, you are here to find the perfect wedding dress and that is a happy occasion, yes?" She smiled at us. "Are you sure there isn't anything else I can get you?"

"Do you make it a habit of leaving the shop when Eva or Vidalia have people in the salons?"

"What?"

"Pepper, that's enough," Mom said. "Let the girl do her job."

The door opened and Vidalia walked in. "Sorry, that was another appointment calling to cancel. I tried to tell them that you were here and very comfortable, but they said they didn't want a murder associated with their dress." She sighed.

Felicity gave Mom a silent look of *See, I told you.*

"Well, um, if there's nothing else I can do for you, I'll

leave you in Vidalia's good hands," Theresa said, and skirted out the door.

"We can give you a nice review online," I offered.

Vidalia looked relieved. "Would you? Only if you really believe I did a good job, though. Now, Felicity, let's try on dress number two. It is probably what you thought you wanted when you came in. Let's see if it still is, okay?"

I moved back to my chair so that Vidalia could take down the next dress. She and Felicity went back behind the screen.

"What was that all about?" Mom whispered to me.

"What?" I snagged a grape.

"You were grilling that poor girl."

"She seems suspicious to me," I said. "Didn't she act suspicious to you?"

"She did seem nervous, but it might be because her job is on the line and you acted as if she might have something to do with Eva's death."

I raised my pale red eyebrows. "Who says she didn't?"

"Stop it. I'm certain Detective Murphy has ruled her out already. Now, did you notice the second dress is the white one? Do you think she is going to talk Felicity into wearing the pale blue one?"

"Maybe." I shrugged. "Let's see how it looks before we get upset, okay?" I patted Mom's knee. She frowned at me. Today she wore a pair of light brown wool slacks, a cotton button-down white blouse that was tailored to her curves, and a brown sweater.

I had on navy slacks with a silky blue-and-white-striped

long-sleeved shirt, a slim gold belt, and polished flats. I never knew when I might have to meet with a client and so I always dressed meeting ready. Besides, Mom had taught us early on that if you wanted good service when you went shopping, you should always dress your best. Shop girls gravitated to people who gave off the appearance of money whether you spent anything or not.

"Okay, ladies, here is the traditional white gown," Vidalia said as Felicity walked out. The gown had a strapless sweetheart neckline. It was pinned tight to the waist and hip but was more of a fit-and-flare style than the traditional mermaid look.

"You look very beautiful," I said carefully.

Felicity stepped up on the dais and studied herself from all angles in the mirror. "It is sort of the shape I was thinking."

"I hear a big *but* in that statement," Mom said as she steepled her fingers.

Felicity made eye contact with us from the mirror. "It does seem like the same dress all the girls are wearing."

"There is nothing wrong with that, if the dress is what you wanted," Vidalia pointed out.

Felicity bit her bottom lip. "It is what I was thinking . . ."

There was a knock at the door and Theresa stuck her head inside. "I'm so sorry to interrupt, Vidalia. It's the Marshal party. They want to cancel their order."

"What? No! We are already on the second fitting."

Theresa's expression was helpless. "I know. I explained

that to them, but they are adamant. I think you need to talk to them directly."

"I'm sorry, this will only take a moment," Vidalia said. "Please take your time discussing this dress. Knock on the door when you are ready to change and Theresa or I will come in and help you." Vidalia left, closing the door behind her.

"Poor thing," Mom muttered. "I can't imagine how she is going to recover from this."

I noticed Felicity still frowning at her reflection. "That's not the dress, is it?"

"No," she said with a sigh. "It's not."

"I'll get Theresa." I opened the door and waved Theresa over. "Felicity is ready to take the dress off."

"Of course." The young woman pushed by me.

I noticed that Vidalia was on the phone and having a very animated discussion. As I went to close the door, a young man walked into the shop. It seemed strange that a guy would come into the bridal shop alone. He didn't have any boxes or bags, so he wasn't a delivery guy.

The young man was dressed in low-hanging jeans and sloppy tennis shoes, and a black hoodie covered his hair, leaving only a pale thin face showing. Vidalia's expression when she spotted the guy had all my warning bells going off. If this was a robbery, I didn't want my family involved. I closed the door until only a partial crack showed and listened as Vidalia hung up the phone. If there was going to be another crime, I wanted to keep my family safe.

Chapter 8

"What do you want, Thad?" Vidalia's tone was decidedly chilly.

Okay, so Vidalia knew the guy, but she wasn't so happy to see him.

"Is Theresa here?" he asked, looking around. I closed the door a little more so as not to be noticed.

"She's working." Vidalia crossed her arms.

"Dude, I need to see her."

"Fine. Wait here." Vidalia headed toward our room and I quickly closed the door and pretended to study the last gown. "I'm so sorry," Vidalia said as she entered the room. "I need Theresa for a moment."

By this time Felicity was out of the second dress. Theresa

was putting the dress on the hanger when she came out from behind the screen.

"What's the matter?" Theresa said as she hung the second dress on the wall peg.

"Thad is here and he's insisting on seeing you." Vidalia expression was stern. "I told him you were working, but he won't leave until he sees you."

Theresa ducked her head and hurried out the door.

"I'm so sorry. This will only take a moment more. Please help yourself to the refreshments. If you need to use the facilities, there is a restroom just down the hall on the left."

She left, closing the door behind her. I took that as my cue to follow on the pretense of finding the restroom. "I'll be right back," I said.

Vidalia was scolding the couple about work boundaries and how Theresa was on the clock and should never be interrupted. I moved down the hall toward the bathroom until I was out of sight but still within hearing range.

"Dude, chill," Thad said. "This will only take a second."

"And that's another thing," Vidalia said firmly. "I am not a dude. My name is Vidalia Denikin. Mrs. Denikin to you."

"Sure," Thad said. He and Theresa moved toward the door, which was closer to me but still out of sight.

"What do you want?" Theresa asked.

"You know what I want," Thad said.

"You can't come in here like this. It looks bad."

"Give me what I want and I'll go away."

"Fine."

I peeked around the corner to see Theresa give Thad

some money. The guy pocketed the cash and gave Theresa a kiss on the cheek.

"You're the best, babe."

He left and I heard Vidalia chastise Theresa. "He cannot come in here. I mean it. He looks like a hoodlum and I need my shop to be above reproach. Especially now. Do you understand?"

"Yes, ma'am," Theresa said.

"Good, now sit at that desk and do your job. I'm going back in and seeing if I can salvage the one appointment we still have."

I hurried to the bathroom door and pretended to be coming out as Vidalia passed the hall. "Trouble?"

She stopped at the sight of me and sighed. "I'm sorry for the interruption. Theresa is a good worker, but she has a terrible time with her choice of men."

"She said she was out sick the day your mother died," I said. "That must have made things crazy here, having no receptionist."

"Not so bad." She shrugged. "I was able to go to the coffee shop and take a much-needed break."

"Oh, that's right. You had coffees in your hands when you came in that day. There weren't any clients here, were there?"

"No, we were swamped that morning. I remember because I had a particularly difficult appointment and I lost her because I had to keep going to answer the door." She frowned. "Sometimes I wish I could hire an extra girl, but that's for the future now."

"Strange, I remember you having three coffees when

you came in," I said. "I have no idea why I would have thought of that."

"I did have three coffees," she said. "My mother loved her coffee. It was never enough to bring her one."

"Huh, I suppose there are some two-fisted coffee drinkers. Did anyone hold a grudge against your mother?"

"Are you asking if she has—I mean had—any enemies? The answer to that is no. Everyone loved her. My mother had an uncanny ability to make every bride happy and soothe the family issues that always come up in wedding situations."

"She must have been an extraordinary woman."

"She was." Tears welled up in Vidalia's eyes. "I told Detective Murphy that I think the motive was a robbery gone wrong."

"Why do you say that?" I drew my brows together in confusion. Detective Murphy didn't let me in on this little tidbit. The last thing I knew, he didn't think it was a robbery because nothing seemed to be missing from the shop.

"We don't keep a lot of money on the premises. Most of our gowns are far too expensive for cash. But when I had a chance to check the inventory, I discovered that the petty cash was missing, along with a couple of our top designer gowns worth thousands."

"Who would buy a stolen wedding gown?"

She shrugged. "People sell gowns on the Internet all the time. I'm certain someone would jump at getting a designer sample gown for a quarter of the price. Even at that price point the thief would make thousands."

"Did you let Detective Murphy know? I mean, they could have someone looking for the stolen dresses listed on the Internet."

"Yes, of course, he said that he has his men keeping an eye on the Internet sites that sell second-hand dresses in case one of mine shows up. Perhaps it will lead them to the killer." She shrugged. "Still, for the dresses to come back in showroom condition is a long shot as you say. I'm better off getting my insurance to pay for it." Vidalia gave a forced laugh. "Come on, let's go inside. I have the perfect dress for your sister and it's time she tried it on."

"Can I ask one more question?"

"Sure," she said, but her tone made it clear she was done being questioned.

"Do you take a coffee break at the shop the same time every day?"

"Of course, it's sort of a thing with me. I like to keep a regular schedule. Are you ready to see your sister in her perfect dress?"

"Of course," I said, and let her lead me into the room. But my thoughts were not on Felicity. They were on the fact that if she took her break the same time every day, the killer may have known that Eva was here alone

* * *

Mom gave me a questioning look when I returned and sat down beside her. I raised an eyebrow, shrugged, and snagged a little cake from the plate.

"I'm so sorry for all the delays, ladies," Vidalia said

as she pulled the last dress from its hook. "Come on, Felicity. Are you ready to see your wedding dress?"

Felicity rolled her eyes at us. "Sure."

They went behind the screen and Mom leaned toward me. "Did you get your answers? Because Felicity has had enough of this place. Once she says no to this dress, we're out of here."

"Yes, I did," I said. "We can go anytime that Felicity wants."

"And here she is, your bride," Vidalia said as Felicity walked out from behind the curtain.

The dress was not pale blue as we first thought, but rather a lovely abalone-colored silk that shimmered in the lightest of blues and pinks and whites. The top was a delicate pale bluish white lace that covered the strapless part of the pearl silk and formed a portrait collar and three-quarter length sleeves. The gown narrowed at the waist then flared slightly, falling to the ground in delicate waves. The skirt had a wrapped train that flowed from the side of the waist to the back of the dress, revealing a panel of white embroidered flowers on the back of the skirt and along the hem of the train.

"Oh!" Mom put her hands to her mouth, her eyes filled with tears.

Felicity stepped up on the dais and froze. She gave the same little gasp as my mother and her eyes also welled up. Watching them made my heart tumble in delight. The dress was perfect.

Vidalia didn't gloat. Instead she snagged a veil from

the tall thin shelves filled with veils and gloves on the wall next to the door and went to work. "And there is our bride," she said, and stepped back with pride.

"Oh, Felicity!" Mom was on her feet and standing beside my sister. I couldn't help but follow.

"It's the dress," Felicity said in an awed whisper.

"It's the dress," Vidalia said with a smile.

"How did you know?" Felicity asked.

"I just do. Like I said, it's a gift."

For the first time that day I knew that Vidalia was telling the absolute truth. My sister was a bride. The reflection of her and my mom and me in the three-way mirror made my heart squeeze. This was the moment dreams were made of and one of many moments I hoped my new career would be able to provide for a lifetime of other women.

Chapter 9

Felicity might have had reservations about buying a dress from Vidalia, but once she found "The Dress" it was all done but the haggling, and Mom was a champion haggler. Vidalia helped Felicity out of the gown and returned with paperwork on pricing and details.

Mom was resolute about the price she was willing to pay. I think both Felicity and Vidalia were in tears by the time Mom finally said, "It's a deal." She had indeed negotiated a deep discount for the dress if we promised to tell everyone where Felicity bought her gown and how wonderful the experience was. It didn't hurt that I also promised that I would include one of Vidalia's business cards in my marketing packet for Perfect Proposals.

"My husband, Anton, is going to think I have lost my

mind," Vidalia stated as she watched Mom sign the agreement and then write the check. "You have the gown at cost plus alterations."

"Warren Evans, Felicity's fiancé, has connections with all of Chicago's high society, doesn't he, dear?" Mom said, and continued without waiting for Felicity to answer. "He's practically the entire reason Pepper's Perfect Proposals business is so successful."

"Well, I'd like to think I had something to do with that," I muttered, and pulled the strap of my purse over my shoulder.

"Plus, you will get free advertising to all of Pepper's clients for the next six months. She deals only in exclusive high-end proposals. Isn't that right, dear? You truly have made the deal of a lifetime." Mom stood up and handed over the check. "We'll see you soon."

"Yes, for fittings and to buy the bridesmaid dresses and mother-of-the-bride dress—if I can afford to sell them to you, of course," she said with a cool smile.

"Of course," Mom trilled, and slung her arms through mine and Felicity's and practically skipped out of the shop.

"Oh, my goodness," Felicity said as we left the shop. "I had no idea it was going to be the one. I'd never felt like a bride before and then . . ." She got choked up again.

I smiled and hugged her shoulder. "You are going to knock Warren's socks off."

"The dress was simply perfect," Mom said with a big grin on her face.

"I thought Vidalia was going to tear her hair out over

your haggling," I teased my mom. "I thought we were trying to save her business not lowball her out of it."

"Please, a lowball sale is a sale and that is what will save her business. She can tell everyone who asks that her business is still strong. After all, she sold a gown today."

"Nice," I said.

"Yes, it is. Remember this when you go dress shopping. Your mother is more than a pretty face." She waggled her eyebrows and tapped her temple with her index finger.

"Of course you are," I said. "We didn't get all our smarts from Dad."

"Shall we go grab some dinner?" Felicity asked.

I glanced at my cell phone. It was nearly six thirty already and my message light blinked. "You two go on without me. I've got to check a few phone messages and I want to write down what I learned today before I forget."

Felicity and Mom exchanged a look that did not go unnoticed.

"What? I'm running a business."

"And your sister liked that plaid bridesmaid dress, didn't you, Felicity?" Mom looked smug.

It was my turn to roll my eyes. "Fine. Where are you going? I'll try to meet you there."

Mom looked at Felicity.

"Lou Malnati's," Felicity said. "I feel like pizza."

"I'll call your father," Mom said.

"The one on Higgins Road?" I asked

"Yes," Felicity said. "Warren is in Schaumburg today working at the satellite office."

"Perfect," I said. "See you there in a few." I strolled to my car, unlocked it, and got inside. Locking the doors, I hit the message button on my smartphone.

"Hello, my name is Toby. I was at the country club and overheard Warren and Felicity talking about their proposal. I'd like to hire Perfect Proposals. Please call me at this number."

Well, that sounded like a nice lead. Especially since I had Mary's proposal nearly all planned and had gotten Alexander's family to agree to hold up the cards for his proposal at the landing zone of his Big Leap event. I dialed the number.

"Hello?"

"Yes, is this Toby? I'm Pepper Pomeroy, the owner of Perfect Proposals. You called and left me a message?"

"Oh, right," he said. "Yes, I understand you've done a couple of unusual romantic proposals."

"Yes, you can go to the Perfect Proposals website and you'll see pictures, testimonials, references, and a link to some of the video clips."

"Oh, I don't need to go to your website. I trust Warren Evans. I want to hire you. Money is no object. Can we meet?"

"Certainly." My heart skipped a beat at the idea that money was no object. I made my fee off a direct percentage of the costs of the proposal, so the bigger the event, the more money I made. Most of which went right back into the business, but it would be nice to have a little extra cash when I went looking for a new apartment.

And I was planning on finding a new apartment soon.

"Please name a date, time, and place and I'll be there so we can get started on the details," I said.

"Great, can you meet me tomorrow, say ten A.M. Does that work?"

"It works," I said. "Where?"

"Meet me at Centre City Books in Forest Park. Do you know where that is?"

"Sure, it's a favorite of my father's," I said. A bookstore was an unusual place for a meeting, but I was game, especially when he reiterated that money was no option. Forest Park wasn't all that far from my parents' home. "How will I know you?"

"I'll be sitting in the right corner reading nook and I'll wear a red carnation in my buttonhole."

"Great, I'll see you tomorrow at ten." I hung up. What an odd character. Who meets in a bookstore and wears a carnation? Most people I dealt with had a LinkedIn profile and posted pictures and their entire background. Come to think of it, he hadn't given me his last name.

I frowned. I suspected it was going to be an interesting meeting.

The next three messages were from my vendors—the baker with the final directions for the black-and-white cake for Mary's engagement party with the *Casablanca* motif, the permits for the jump site for Alexander's Big Leap, and the pilot of the jump plane clearing his flight plan.

Happy to have a thriving business, I glanced over at the dress shop. Vidalia stepped outside and waited to lock up. She looked satisfied with the sale. She really did have a flair for finding the right dress—at least Felicity's dress. It would not be hard to recommend her to my clients.

I chewed on my bottom lip as I noted that Theresa walked out after her. The girl headed in the opposite direction. There was something going on with that girl, or her boyfriend at the very least. It was a good thing Felicity bought her dress there. It meant a couple of fitting appointments, and of course, the opportunity to go back and buy bridesmaid dresses and mom's mother-of-the-bride gown.

It also meant that I would have more opportunities to ask Vidalia and Theresa questions that Detective Murphy would never think to ask.

Chapter 10

❧

Ten A.M. the next morning, I opened the door to the bookstore. It had a classic glass front, a red awning with white type that said Centre City Books, and brick on the rest of the old-fashioned building. I entered to the warm aroma of books and coffee—two of my favorite scents. A smile came to my face at the realization that it had been a while since I'd visited a bookstore and experienced firsthand that wonderful smell.

I found Toby in the right-hand corner as he had promised. He looked to be in his mid to late forties and of average height and build. He had a full head of dark, wavy hair and a five-o'clock shadow, which was a bit odd for ten in the morning.

I tilted my head and squinted my eyes. If he were

spiffed up, he could be good-looking in an older George Clooney kind of way. Unfortunately he was as rumpled as that funny old television detective, the one I used to watch reruns of with my father. What was his name? Hmmm—Columbus? Colom . . . Oh, right, Columbo. Anyway, even though he had pinned a red carnation to his shirt—with a safety pin, mind you—he was not at all sophisticated. He wore a T-shirt with Wile E. Coyote on it, droopy jeans with completely frayed hems, and ripped white skateboarder shoes.

"Hi, Toby?"

He looked up and I stuck out my hand.

"Pepper Pomeroy of Perfect Proposals."

"Right," he said and stood, taking my hand and giving it a quick shake. "So, you're a redhead."

"Yes," I said with a nod. It was usually the first thing people noticed about me. The next was my long, thin Olive Oyl frame. "Shall we get some coffee and talk?"

"No need for coffee," he said. "If you don't mind, I'm interested in the movies." He took me to the back where the wall of movie racks sat. Strangely he went right to the B-movie action-adventure DVDs and started stacking them up on his arm.

"Um, okay." I watch as he pulled at least five out at random, but flipped past others. Then I noticed one I'd actually seen. "Hey, that one was pretty good," I said in an effort to be helpful.

"Got it," Toby said. "I own most of these. I'm looking to fill the gaps with the ones I don't have."

"Right, okay, so about the proposal," I pulled my pen and notepad out of my purse and wrote his name across the top. "Wait, I'm sorry, what is your last name?"

"Mallard, Toby Mallard, with two *l*'s." He pointed at my notebook.

"Thanks, Toby Mallard with two *l*'s. Now, what kind of proposal are you thinking of?"

"Oh, something out of this world, you know, romantic and magical and certain to make my love say *yes, yes, yes*." He didn't even look at me as he continued to peruse the movies.

"Okay, well, what kinds of things does your, er, love think are romantic?"

"Oh, you know, the usual stuff."

I winced and wrote down usual stuff. "Well, see, that's a problem. I deal in the unusual stuff. For instance, Warren Evans proposed to his bride-to-be in a private plane filled with memorabilia from their dating life."

"I know. I heard them tell Amy Hanson all about it."

"Then there's the guy who did this scuba proposal because he and his fiancée loved to travel and scuba together. I have a client right now with a parachuting proposal. Do you see how it's the unusual and grand gesture that makes it a Perfect Proposal? It's something that you and your love do together that binds you to one another and reflects the type of couple you are."

"Right."

This wasn't working. "How long have you been going out?"

"The usual amount of time," he said.

"Okay, how old is she?"

"The right age for me."

I was really getting frustrated. "Can you at least tell me her name?"

"Her name is Laura."

That was something. I wrote it down. "Good, Laura, that's good."

Toby continued to shop, not making eye contact. I tried to remain professional. I had a bad feeling that he might be wasting my time.

"What kind of hobbies does Laura have?"

He shrugged. "Girl hobbies, you know, shopping and such."

"Does she like to shop for anything in particular? For example, you have an action/adventure movie collection—"

"How did you know that?" He frowned.

I pointed to the stack in his hands. "You told me."

"Huh." He glanced down at his hands then moved on to looking through the vinyl album section. I presumed he was a vinyl record album fan. Some people collected old records because they swore the sound was better than the new digital recordings. I was happy not to have stacks of records in my house collecting dust. All my music was stored online.

The vinyl album section was thankfully smaller than the movie section. There was a long silence while he quickly went through the records. Clearly he wasn't going to answer the last question. Time to be more direct.

"Does she collect anything? Anything at all? Dolls, elephants, cookie jars?"

"I doubt it." He frowned as he pulled out an old Guns N' Roses album, flipped it over, read the songs, and put it back.

Time to quit being nice and get down to brass tacks. "What is it that you want to hire me for?"

"I need a girl's point of view," he said as he dug through the old covers. "You know, I want a fancy restaurant, but I'm not really into that, so I need someone to pick one out."

"You want me to pick out a fancy restaurant?"

"Yes, and I want the place decorated with Laura's favorite flowers . . . whatever those are."

"You need me to find out and book her favorite restaurant and order her favorite flowers?"

"Oh, and I want the place all to ourselves."

"Buying out an entire restaurant will be quite costly."

"I told you money was not a problem. It's the details and such."

"What if it cost, oh, I don't know, fifty thousand dollars?" I threw a big number out there to test him.

He didn't even flinch. "Okay," he said, and moved on to the books. "Oh, and I need you to pick out a ring."

"Pick out an engagement ring," I stated and wrote *nuts* in my notebook. "Do you know her ring size? What kind of stone she wants? What cut she prefers?"

"That's what I'm paying you for," he said.

"How am I supposed to do any of that if I don't know

anything about Laura?" Seriously, was I supposed to become a private detective?

He stopped shopping and looked at me. "I'm rich. Like very rich. Make it happen for me, okay?"

I was so frustrated I'd decided to quote him triple my current rate. Let's see how rich he really is. "Fine, can I see a picture of Laura?"

"What's that going to do?"

"It will allow me to see her style, her coloring, so I can help with the ring." I half wondered if he was making the whole thing up.

"Okay." He pulled out a top-of-the-line iPhone and scrolled through it. "Here. This is Laura."

He showed me a picture of a gorgeous young woman who looked to be in her late twenties or early thirties. She was slim, dark haired, and the photo looked like it had been taken when she was crossing a marathon finish line. Sweaty and all, she was still beautiful.

"Where does she work?" I asked. She looked like a model or a television personality. If that were the case, I might be able to find out more about her online.

"She's a partner at Marley and Thomas, LLC. It's a law firm."

"Yes, I know the firm." They handled all the big political cases in Chicago. "I thought I recognized her." Most likely I had seen her on television after all.

"You can't visit her at work. No one gets in there without an appointment."

"I bet," I said, and frowned. "Wait, you can. How about

you bring me in to meet her and I'll pretend that I'm just a friend."

He shook his head. "Won't work."

"Lunch then, you can tell her you went to college with me and I'm in town for a day and you want her to meet me."

"No."

"How am I supposed to meet her?"

"I'm sure you'll come up with something." He went to the cashier to pay for his stack of purchases.

"That's going to take time and I get paid by the hour," I said. "In fact, I'll need a retainer up front."

"I figured," he said, and fished his wallet out of his back pocket. "I got you a cashier's check." He pulled out a folded check and handed it to me.

I opened the check and blinked at the amount. I confirmed that it was a cashier's check made out to Perfect Proposals.

"I assume that will cover your down payment," he said, and pushed his movies and books toward the bored-looking kid behind the counter.

"Yes," I said as I stared at the check. "This will cover it."

"Good. I look forward to hearing your ideas." He paid the bill, and when he put his credit card back in his wallet, he pulled out a card and handed it to me. "You can reach me here." He gathered up his bags. "Talk to you soon."

I watched him leave the bookstore and looked back down at the check. It was for ten thousand dollars. He hadn't even asked me to sign a contract or a quote or put in a bid.

"You okay, honey?" The manager came up to the counter. She was a middle-aged woman who studied me through her cat-eyed reading glasses.

"Yes, I am, thanks." I carefully put the check in my purse along with my notebook and pen, and pushed through the bookstore door. Toby might turn out to be a difficult client, but every business owner had their price, and right now mine was going straight to the bank.

Chapter 11

I stopped by Gage's prop warehouse on my way back to my apartment. Well, it wasn't exactly on the way, but I was in a happy mood. The moment I had gotten in my car, I drove straight to an ATM machine and deposited that check. There was no way I was going to be robbed with a ten-thousand-dollar cashier's check in my purse. I'm sure it would take a few days to process, but at least it was in a safe place.

Don't get me wrong, Mom had been correct when she told Vidalia that Warren had helped me start Perfect Proposals, but this was my first big client check. I still didn't quite believe it. In fact the whole thing was so odd, it certainly felt too good to be true. If Todd decided he wanted his money back, or I discovered I couldn't figure out how to make his proposal perfect, I could still give him a refund. If I lost the check or worse—got mugged—then I would be in a bad, bad place.

I parked in the lot at the side of the warehouse, checked my hair, slicked on some fresh lipstick, and went to see Gage. The prop warehouse catered to the Chicago theater and movie scene. Many movies were shot in town, and we had a very active commission for the arts that ensured we were, if not world-class, then nationally known for our theater and film support.

The doors were rigged with bells that went off when you crossed the threshold. There was a young guy sitting at the desk that served as a reception area. He looked about nineteen with floppy light brown hair, a generous nose, dark brown eyes, and a thin build.

"Hi," I said.

He put down his graphic novel. "Hey."

I stood for a moment, awkwardly expecting him to ask if he could help me. Finally, I gave in and spoke. "Right, I'm looking for Gage. Is he around?"

"Sure." The kid went back to his novel.

I guess that was my cue to go back into the warehouse proper and look for my boyfriend. Gage had taken me through the place a couple of times with my first two jobs, but I had followed him like a little puppy, not really paying that much attention to where we were going and how we got there. That happened sometimes when I was around a handsome guy.

"So, he's in the back?" I asked, and pointed to the door that led to the rest of the warehouse.

"Yep."

I moved my gaze from the kid to the door and back a couple of times, shrugged, and made my way into the back. The bay doors must have been open because there was the distinctive smell of diesel from a truck. I heard the *beep, beep* sound of someone backing up a forklift. It was a lot dimmer in the huge warehouse than in the front office reception space. I stood there a moment, waiting for my eyes to adjust.

Between the scent of dust, the diesel, the dimness, and the beeping of the forklift, I found it difficult to get my bearings. Someone put their hand on my shoulder and I may have screamed a little.

"Whoa, it's okay, it's me," Gage said with a big grin.

I put my hand on my racing heart. "You scared me silly. My heart is going a mile a minute."

"I'd rather it was desire that got your heart racing," he teased, and kissed my cheek. "It's nice to see you. What brings you by the old prop house?" He waved his hand at the racks of warehoused furniture and crazy props of all shapes and sizes. Just for the treasure hunting alone, I'd love to have the time to go through the place. It was like the city's giant attic.

"I came to see you, mostly." I kissed him back and smiled.

"Now that's the kind of thing a man likes to hear from

a beautiful woman. Let's go into my office and get out of the dust and the noise." He put his hand on the small of my back and I got all gooey inside. There was something so nice about walking beside him and feeling the heat of his body.

At work Gage wore a pale blue, long-sleeved, button-down shirt with *Prop House* embroidered over the front pocket. The collar was open showing a snow white V-neck tee underneath. I wanted so bad to bury my nose in the little vee and inhale the scent of cotton T-shirt warmed by clean male with a hint of aftershave. Loose-fitting jeans and Top-Sider shoes finished his uniform.

I was thankful I'd checked my hair, which was in a neat—well as neat as curly red hair could ever be—low ponytail at the base of my neck. Today I wore a floaty floral top over a cotton tank dress and wedge sandals that made me nearly as tall as Gage, who was six foot two.

His office was to the right of the door at the front of the warehouse, so it faced the long rows of shelves and you could almost see the open bay doors. "Have a seat." He waved toward a plastic chair in front of his desk. "Can I get you some coffee or a bottle of water?"

"Yes," I said with a short laugh. "I just met with a new client and was expecting at least coffee, but it didn't happen."

"No?" he asked as he snagged two mugs from the side credenza in his office.

"No, and I was willing to buy, even." I shook my head at the memory of the odd encounter with Toby.

Gage poured coffee from a small eight-cup drip maker. "I just made this so it's fresh. Creamer?"

"Yes, please," I said as I took the warm mug. The room filled with the rich scent of coffee. "Oh, the good stuff," I said as I sipped and held out my hand for the two liquid half-and-half servings he gave me.

"I'm not much into house blends," he said with a laugh.

"I figured," I said. The coffee was definitely not the standard coffeehouse brew. "No Keurig?"

"Naw, I'm still old-fashioned enough to like a pot of coffee."

"I agree. There's something about seeing the full pot sitting there ready for you and watching it being poured into your cup. Gosh, I sound like a nostalgic old person." I giggled at the thought.

He sat on the edge of his desk and sent me a look. "You really like your coffee."

"I've spent a lot of late nights with just me and my coffeepot."

"So tell me about this new client," he nudged.

"I don't know what to think." I shook my head. "It's why I stopped by. The whole thing is odd and I wanted to talk to someone about it."

"Okay." He sipped and studied me with his warm gaze.

"I got a call from this guy, Toby, who said he overheard Warren and Felicity talking about their proposal at the country club."

"Sounds good so far."

"We set up an appointment at his local bookstore, Centre City Books. Do you know it?"

"I've heard about it." He tilted his head, his gaze intent.

"I get there expecting to get some coffee and talk. Instead I find him. He wore a red carnation—"

"Really?"

"Yeah, it was safety pinned to his T-shirt."

"His T-shirt?"

"Yes." We shared a smile. "I introduced myself and he got up, asked me to follow him, and started shopping."

"Shopping?" Gage raised his left brow and took a sip of coffee.

"Right? He pulled an armful of old B action movies from the DVD section. He never made eye contact as he told me he wanted to ask his 'love' "—I made air quotes around the word *love*—"to marry him and he wanted me to pull out all the stops. But when I asked him some questions about his girlfriend, he wouldn't or couldn't tell me anything about her."

"Nothing?"

"Well, when I pressed him, I got her first name. And he had a picture of her running a marathon. Come to think of it, I should have asked him if he had any photos of them together."

"I don't have any photos of us together," Gage said with a twinkle in his eye.

"Really?" I scrunched my brow. "We've know each other for years."

"And you were with Bobby the entire time."

"Oh, well, we'll take care of that right now." I got up and wiggled in close to him, he put his arm around me, and I rested my head on his shoulder. "Smile," I urged as I held out my phone and took two quick snapshots. "I'll—"

He snagged my chin with his index finger and kissed me on the lips. The kiss was soft and warm and nearly perfect. In my surprise I made an *oh* sound and he took advantage to deepen the kiss.

Well, then, I thought. Since that was so nice, I wrapped my arms around his neck and kissed him back until my toes curled. Someone knocked on the window of his office and catcalled loud enough that we could hear it through the glass.

"Okay," I said, and stepped back. "Wow."

He sat there grinning.

My cheeks flamed bright red. I knew this because the heat in them was intense and I couldn't stop the pinchy smile that always came on when I was embarrassed. Being a redhead, every emotion showed on my skin. I distracted myself by looking at the pictures on my phone. They were really quite good. "I'll text these to you."

"Thanks," he said, and picked his coffee cup back up. "You were telling me that there was something off about this client."

"Right." I sat back down after sending the text. "Toby, that's his name."

"You told me that," he said, and nodded. "Go on."

"He finally gave me his girlfriend's full name. She's a

high-powered attorney with that law firm that represents the politicians and other politicos here. He told me there was no way I could contact her at work, and I believe him. A law firm that big has all kinds of gatekeepers to keep the press out. So I asked him to take me to lunch with her, you know, introduce me as his friend. He refused."

"This guy wants you to do a proposal for a woman, but he only has a snapshot of her running a marathon and knows nothing else about her?"

"Weird, right?"

"He's lying to you," Gage said, and crossed his arms. "A guy in love would tell you all kinds of things about the woman of his dreams . . . like the way her red hair glints in the sunlight or the fact that she likes two creams in her coffee or that she looks spectacular in florals . . ."

The heat returned to my cheeks. "That's what I thought. I figured he was a kook and I was going to turn him down, but then he said he was very rich and that money was no object."

"Lie."

"I agree. I told him that I needed a retainer deposit before I'd do any kind of in-depth work."

"Smart."

"I even gave him a ridiculous 40 percent fee for services."

"And that didn't make any difference? I'd run not walk away from this one."

"Except he handed me a cashier's check made out to Perfect Proposals for ten grand."

Gage turned his head slightly and eyed me through narrowed eyes. "Ten thousand dollars?"

"Yes, and he told me he was looking forward to the ideas I'd come up with. Then he paid for his movies and a few books and walked out."

"What did you do?" His brows pulled together.

"I deposited that check in the nearest ATM machine." I let out an uncomfortable laugh. "I wasn't going to take the chance of losing it."

"Was it a real check?"

"It appeared real. I'll know in a few days when it posts to my account."

"Wow, okay. So you're stuck helping this guy."

"It was ten grand, Gage. Should I have chased him down and refused it? I mean, what if it is only the tip of what I can make? He told me twice that money was no option. He's very rich and apparently used to people doing things for him."

I picked up the mug that I had absently left on the desk when I had gotten up to snap the picture and wrapped my hands around its warmth.

"No, no," Gage said, "taking the check was fine. So was depositing it."

"It's going to clear, right? Because it's a cashier's check."

"It should clear, yes." His expression still looked puzzled. "What are you going to do?"

"I'm going to do some digging online first, I guess. If Laura has a Facebook page or at the very least a LinkedIn presence or something . . ." I put down the mug and dug around in my purse, pulled out my notebook and pen, and wrote down, *Check for Laura's Facebook page.* "I'll have to ask Toby if he has a Facebook page. That way if her privacy settings are what I suspect they are, I can connect to Toby's page and at least see her posts on his feed. Maybe I can get her to friend me."

Gage shook his head. "I doubt an attorney of her caliber has anything personal on the Web. With their clientele there's too much of a chance for anyone to hack it."

"Right." I frowned. "Maybe I can search her LinkedIn for hints."

"Again . . ."

"She probably only has a professional face online," I finished.

"Exactly."

I sat back and frowned. "I'm going to have to try to meet her in person." I sighed. "Or"—I raised my eyebrows—"I could get to know her paralegal or secretary and see if I can get any good gossip from them."

Gage nodded. "Now there you might have a shot."

"Thanks," I said, and stood, suddenly all my focus on finding out more about Toby's Laura.

"You're welcome," Gage said. "Was there anything you needed from the warehouse? We're getting a new truckload tomorrow. There was a big Northshore estate sale and I picked up some really cool things. Want to come by in a couple of days and go through it with me? There might be some stuff you can use for your next event."

"Yes!" I said, excitement curling through me. Who could say no to any reason to spend time with Gage?

"Great, so we're good? Bobby didn't freak you out too much?"

"No." I shook my head. "In fact, I've been looking for a new place. So if you hear of anything good with decent rent . . ."

"I'll let you know." He took a step toward me. "Unless you want to just move in with me."

I froze. "What?"

"Just kidding." He kissed my temple and turned me to face him. "Seriously, I don't want to rush you. I know you're trying to figure out who Pepper is. I don't mind the wait."

Relief washed over me. I smiled. "It's not that living with you and having you around when I come home at night wouldn't be great."

"It's not time yet," he said softly. "Like I said, I'm willing to wait. Heck, I've waited for you since high school. What's another year or two in the grand scheme of things?"

"Well, gosh, I hope it doesn't take me years to find myself." I wrapped my arms around his neck and planted a firm kiss on his mouth. "Here in your arms is a good start."

"I'd like to think so, too."

I grinned up at him. "I'll let you get back to work. Thanks for the coffee and for letting me bounce the whole strange Toby thing off you. It's good to get a guy's perspective."

"Good luck with that," he said, and opened the office door for me. "See you in a couple days."

"Get back to work," I scolded, and headed out with a

smile on my face. It came from the fact that he had a little red lipstick mark on the corner of his mouth. I'd let one of the guys point it out. It never hurt for a girl to leave the guy she liked with a little reminder.

* * *

I left Gage and got in my car to see that Detective Murphy had left me a voice mail. He was most likely returning my call. I'd phoned him to discuss what I'd learned about Vidalia when Felicity had purchased her wedding dress.

"This is Detective Murphy," he answered on the third ring.

"Hi, Detective Murphy," I said as I pulled out into traffic. "This is Pepper Pomeroy. I saw that you called me."

"Are you driving and talking on your cell?" His tone was accusatory.

"You're on speaker," I said with a soft smile at the father-like tone in his voice. "I've got both hands on the wheel."

"Good. You called me and said you had more information on Eva Svetkovska."

"A few more details, yes."

"I'm listening."

I could picture him in his office doing paperwork and a million other things while I spoke. "Vidalia said the third coffee was for her mother. Which is weird, don't you think?"

"A little . . ."

"Also, she claims to have had time to talk with the barista and then enjoy a full cup before buying herself another cup and two cups for her mother and returning to the store. It's almost as if she were waiting for something to happen."

"People do odd things, Pepper."

"Did you know that Vidalia has an assistant named Theresa?"

"Yes, we interviewed her. She was out sick that day."

"So she says." I hit my blinker and pulled into the center lane to turn left. "But remember Vidalia had brought back three cups of coffee. Did Theresa tell you when she got sick? Was it first thing in the morning or later in the day?"

"Something to consider," he murmured, and I heard him pushing papers.

"Theresa has a boyfriend named Thad who came in while we were there. He put up a fuss until Vidalia got Theresa and the two talked for a bit, and then Theresa gave him money to go away."

"Again, interesting but nothing I can act on," he said, and I heard him pause and take a sip from what I assumed was the perennial coffee cup at his elbow.

"There's something going on with Theresa and Thad, is all I'm saying."

"Are you implying that perhaps Vidalia paid her assistant and her assistant's boyfriend to murder her own mother?"

"It's one way to gain sole ownership of the shop," I said, and headed down the side street to the left of the very same bridal shop. I had decided to revisit the place on the pretense of giving Vidalia my ideas on bridesmaid dresses that did not include plaid.

"Anything else?" He didn't sound very impressed with my findings.

"Vidalia said that some things were stolen, maybe Eva caught Theresa and Thad stealing and when she confronted them, Thad took out the knife, pushed Eva into the alley and killed her."

"Again a theory, any proof?"

"No," I said and pouted. "How's your daughter? Have you talked to her yet?"

"Yeah, no," he said with a short sigh. "She's still with him. I took your advice and haven't said anything."

"But you've done a background check on him, haven't you?" I figured Detective Murphy was a lot like my dad, and if he had access to background information—which he did—then he'd use it. "What did you find? Anything to worry about?"

"No," he said, "nothing outstanding."

"Well, that's good. Trust her," I encouraged. "It's the best way to handle things."

"Okay, Pepper, I've got to go. Call me if you get anything more concrete. And stay out of trouble, okay?"

"I'm trying," I said, and pulled into the parking lot next to Vidalia's bridal shop. I hung up and studied the shop for a moment. The brick false front of the building didn't look any different than a thousand other brick buildings with false fronts that were built in the early 1900s.

I parked Old Blue, my giant Oldsmobile that had belonged to my grandma Mary and was then passed down to me. It had hand-crank windows and locks that needed a key to open, but it was free and rode smooth on the sometimes pothole-crazy Chicago streets. Being a redhead there was no hiding, even in a car. So having a classic Oldsmobile was simply a cheap way to get around. How many people could say they had a twenty-year-old car that had had one owner and only ten thousand miles on it?

Besides, I loved the soft leather seats and the funky tape player. At least it wasn't an 8-track tape deck. That would be a bit over the top even for me.

I got out, hitched my purse over my shoulder, closed and locked my door, then went inside the bridal shop. Vidalia was at the front desk talking angrily on the phone in a language I didn't understand. Chicago was home to a wide variety of immigrants and children of immigrants. That meant that on any given day you could hear five or more languages just walking down the street.

"I have to go. I have a client." Vidalia switched to English and hung up.

"Is everything okay?" I asked as innocently as possible.

"Yes." Vidalia waved her hand dismissively. "It was my brother. He is angry because we read my mother's will today. She left the shop to me alone, while she gave him a small cash inheritance. He thinks he's entitled to more."

"Why would your mother not leave you equal amounts?" The concept was foreign to me. My parents had always made a point of ensuring that Felicity and I were treated the same as much as possible.

"Do not worry. My brother is fine on his own. My

mother knew this and left me the shop. Besides, Vladimir's wife refused to have anything to do with the shop. She feels she is too good to work."

"Oh," I said. "Well, I hope that you work things out with your brother."

"It will be fine," Vidalia said and came around the desk, all business. "We will work it out. He is my brother. We always do. Now, you are here to discuss your bridesmaid dress, yes? Where is your sister?"

"Felicity is working. I came alone to narrow the search. I just want to stress, please no plaid."

She narrowed her mouth. "Of course not. Who would do such a thing? Plaid. No. Come with me."

Relief washed over me when I saw how upset she was by the very idea of plaid. I wouldn't tell Mom or Felicity. I'd let Vidalia do her thing with them, but it was such a relief to know I didn't have to worry that she would think it was a great idea.

I smiled at Theresa, who was in the hall arranging gowns on a rack. The young girl's gaze did not meet mine. She seemed overly busy, as if my presence made her nervous.

Vidalia took me to the back kitchen. I noted that the alley door was boarded up. "Oh," I said as we walked by it.

"It is necessary for now. The fire department is not happy, but I will pay the fine and I told the fire marshal that as well. I need a few months before I look into that alley again. There has never been a fire. I am not worried about fire."

For a moment I thought she was going to spit on the door, but instead she walked quickly past it and into a small room off the kitchen in the back. There were racks of sample bridesmaid dresses.

"Your sister did not tell me her wedding colors. But the dress is pearl, which will be enhanced by pinks, blues, and peaches. I will recommend these colors." She went straight to one rack, then paused and eyed my hair. "No pink for you, though. That is fine. The maid of honor should have a different color dress. How many bridesmaids?"

Theresa walked in and grabbed two dresses and walked out.

"There are four of us in total. Me and Felicity's best friend, Peggy. Then there is Warren's sister, Whitney, and Felicity's friend Susan."

"Hair colors and shapes?" Vidalia was very direct with her questions.

"Um, let's see, dark brown for Peggy and she is a lot like Felicity in shape. Whitney is taller with model curves and wheat blond hair. Susan is also blond and taller than Felicity and Peggy but not as tall as Whitney or me."

"So all over the place." She frowned. Theresa walked in again and, without even excusing herself, cut between Vidalia and myself to snag two more dresses off the rack. "We can match color or we can match style or we can simply match hemline and shoes and such. Thankfully weddings are far more eclectic today. Bridesmaids should be dressed appropriately for each woman so that she does not stick out or take away from the bride. Like a floral arrangement, you must use the proper colors and greenery to complement the lead flower."

Vidalia went back to the rack.

"How is Theresa to work with?" I asked as Vidalia looked through the dresses in front of her.

"She is fine. My mother hired her." Vidalia pulled out a pale blue Grecian draped dress and held it against me to check the hem length, which was just below my knee. "Perhaps this dress," she mused, and turned back to the rack, her hands pushing the hangers quickly from one side to the other.

"Would you hire Theresa?" I asked.

"Theresa is a good worker, but she trusts no one . . . except for that Thad." Vidalia looked like she wanted to spit again but respect for the expensive dresses kept her from doing it.

"You sound as if you wish she didn't trust Thad," I suggested.

"Thad is not my business." Vidalia took out a ballet-inspired number with a mid-length hem and halter top. "Better," she said as she held it up against me. She hung both dresses on a single rack. Then dug through some more. "This is it." She pulled out a satin jewel-toned dress with a high portrait collar, a nipped-in waist, and an A-line skirt. "Try this on."

She handed me the dress and I took it awkwardly. "Um, where?"

"Behind that curtain," She pointed to a sheet that hung

from rings that were pulled through a silver bar, which hung from the ceiling.

I went behind the sheet, noticing the pegs on the wall to hang my stuff, and as I stripped out of my clothes, I talked nervously. "I was wondering . . ."

"Yes?" Vidalia said between the sounds of hangers being pushed on metal racks.

"Do you always go for coffee at the same time every day?" I hung up my dress and was happy to be wearing the slip under it.

"Yes, I told you I like my routine," Vidalia replied, her tone implying that I should remember. "But some days we have client appointments all day. Those days we go whenever we have an opportunity. Why?"

I pulled the beautiful gown over my head and adjusted it around my waist. "You said the store was robbed. I thought perhaps the killer had been watching you and knew when you would leave for coffee."

"It is possible, but not likely. How would they know that that particular day is not filled with appointments?" Vidalia asked as I zipped the side zipper, cinching the dress to my waist, and walked out. Vidalia's gaze lit up. "Yes, that is the dress. I am once again reminded that I have my mother's eye for gowns."

I stepped over to a full-length mirror that rested against the wall. The gown gave me curves that I didn't have. The portrait collar was stiff and tall, giving the illusion of wider shoulders. This narrowed my waist and the flare of the skirt accentuated my hips. "Wow."

"Yes, it is good." Vidalia nodded and fluffed the skirt a little. "A simple pearl belt here at the waist." She touched my waist with both hands. "This will tie in to the bride's gown, complementing but not overshadowing."

The hem of the dress was just below the knee. I could see how the gown would complement all figures and still allow the bride's gown to shine.

"Are you as good at picking coffee as you are at dresses?" I kidded.

"Better." Vidalia winked. "I am even better at making coffee. You should ask my husband, Anton."

I made a little twirl in front of the mirror and watched the fabric whirl around my knees.

"All right, off with the dress. We will surprise your mother and sister when next we see them, yes?"

"Yes," I said, and headed back to the sheet. As I ducked behind and unzipped, I said, "Strange, though, that we were both in the same coffee shop that day. We probably walked right by you. What a coincidence, don't you think?"

"Yes," she said from the other side of the curtain. "A strange coincidence indeed. We must have missed each other, though I would have remembered a redhead."

Chapter 12

I had gotten out of a meeting with the Music Box Theatre to finalize the details for Mary's proposal when my phone rang with an alert. The cashier's check Toby gave me had cleared. The Perfect Proposals business account was now ten thousand dollars fatter.

It was exciting in a nerve-racking sort of way. There was simply so much that didn't feel right about Toby and his Laura. Parking Old Blue in my apartment slot, I frowned at the bar across the street. I had been so busy with everything that I hadn't put a solid effort into finding a new place to rent.

The first glance at online rental listings had shown me a handful of places with great clubhouses and fitness rooms, but I wasn't a big fan of the giant complexes. I really preferred the smaller quaint buildings and two- to four-story walk-ups. That meant that if I was going to get serious about finding a new place, I needed to get a Realtor involved. Except I didn't know any Realtors. I got out of my car, locked it, and headed up to my apartment.

First things first, I should make some lunch and sit down at my laptop to do some research. Besides finding a Realtor and looking at apartments, I needed to figure out what I was going to do with Toby.

Half an hour later I had a turkey sandwich and a salad on the little table next to my laptop. I'd given up on Realtors and sent a text to Felicity and Mom asking for any suggestions. My phone rang immediately.

"Perfect Proposals," I answered.

"What do you need a Realtor for?" Mom asked without even saying hello. "Are you going to get a real office?"

"Hi, Mom," I said, and leaned back in my desk chair. "How are you?"

"I'm good. Now tell me why you need a Realtor. You're not looking at buying a house, are you? I'm not so certain that's a good idea when you are in a start-up situation with your business."

"I want a new apartment," I said, and looked out the window. "Maybe one with a home office." I wasn't going to tell her it was because I lived too close to Bobby's favorite bar.

"Oh, so you aren't going to get a storefront? Because I think it would be better if you considered a little place like the dress shop. That way people could walk in off the street if they saw your shop name."

"I understand, Mom, but I don't think I'm ready for that kind of commitment yet. Right now, Perfect Proposals is a lean home-based business. It's more personal that way. But it would be nice to have a dedicated office in my place."

"Okay." She seemed to pout over the phone. "How is your business doing? Is there a reason you don't want an outside office?"

"Business is good, Mom." I rolled my eyes. "I have three clients right now."

"Good," she said. "Mrs. Piekanski's daughter Mitzy is a Realtor. She specializes in homes in the suburbs. Let me look up her number, hold on."

"Thanks," I muttered, and picked up my pen.

"Mitzy has her own office outside her home," Mom said. I ignored the jab. Mom was a love, but she was very good at driving a point home. "Her number is 847-555-1234."

"Got it. Thanks, Mom."

"How did your client like the idea of the family holding up the 'Will You Marry Me?' cards as he and his girl parachuted down to earth?"

"He loved it," I said. "His family was also very excited by the idea."

"Just his family?"

"No, hers as well," I was more specific. "Both families, Mom, both families can't wait."

"Good. Did Felicity tell you that we have an appointment Saturday with all the bridesmaids to look at dresses?"

"Vidalia did, actually," I said. "I stopped by there to ask another question."

"You did?"

"There are no new breaks in the case," I said. "Listen, Mom, thanks for Mitzy's number. I have to go. See you Saturday?"

"At one P.M.," Mom said. "I'll tell your father you said hi."

"Love you," I said as she hung up. A quick call to Mitzy's number and I left a voice mail expressing who I was and what I was looking for. Heck, it wouldn't hurt to try one of those basement apartments that so many bungalow owners were creating for extra income. I'd miss my second-floor view, but then there was the fact that Bobby wouldn't be able to watch my window from his seat at the bar. That seemed like a good trade-off.

* * *

It turns out Toby Mallard really was a wealthy man. According to my Internet search engine he was a franchise genius specializing in local cable companies and fast-food restaurant investments. An article in the local business trade magazine praised his innate ability to pick the right franchise in the right neighborhood and then hire the right management.

There was a quote from one of his fast-food managers: "Toby Mallard is the perfect hands-off boss. When he hires, he hires the perfect guy for the job and then gets out of his way."

I suppose I should feel flattered that he picked me and

my business. From what I could tell the Toby I met in the bookstore was the real Toby—throwing around money and expecting results with little action on his own part.

I had the nagging feeling that he considered marriage the same as a franchise. Pick the girl, pick the event planner, and become engaged. I certainly hoped I was wrong. It would have made me much more comfortable to have seen a picture or two with Toby and Laura together.

That made me think of the pictures I took of Gage and me. A smile came to my face as I picked up my phone and scrolled through the gallery to the pictures of us in his office. A warm feeling came over me and I sighed. I had the distinct feeling that I was really falling for Gage, and we hadn't even gone out on that many dates yet. If I could fall so easily for him, I really must have been over Bobby years ago.

Why had I not seen that?

That thought made me remember Detective Murphy's daughter. I wished I could meet her and tell her that she deserved a guy who took care of her instead of her being the one to take care of him.

I shook off my musings and sent a text to Gage to let him know I was thinking of him and looked forward to our getting together at the warehouse tomorrow.

He texted back immediately with a smile emoticon and the words, "Thinking of you, too. Can't wait."

I forced myself to put the phone down. I was a grown-up now with a business that needed my attention.

Toby's Laura was indeed a prestigious lawyer. I checked

her LinkedIn profile and found only a brief sketch of her professional qualifications. I went to the firm's page and it, too, was a bare-bones listing of the partners' names and some of the many awards they had won.

Next I checked Twitter and Facebook. Laura had accounts on both, but they were extremely private, allowing me to only see that she was indeed a lawyer. Interestingly enough, her Facebook profile was the same picture that Toby had on his cell phone.

It could mean that he was the one who took the picture and he had sent it to her. Or it could mean that Toby had copied it from her Facebook page. Either way I was unable to see a connection between Toby and Laura anywhere.

Chewing on my bottom lip, I searched for Toby on Facebook and Twitter. He didn't have an account on either social media page. I tried a few others: Tumblr, Reddit, Flicker, Myspace, Blogger . . . nothing.

I went back to Laura's LinkedIn profile, scanning her volunteer areas as well as her hobbies. Nothing seemed to match with what I knew about Toby. I couldn't help it. My instincts were warning me that something was off. Ten thousand dollars or not, there was something very wrong here.

I picked up the phone and dialed the law firm's general number.

"Marley and Thomas LLC, this is Heather, how can I help you?"

"Hi, yes, my name is Pepper Pomeroy. I would like to speak to Laura Walsh."

"I'm sorry. Laura is in a meeting. Can I take a message?"

"I'd rather you send me to her voice mail," I said. "It's kind of personal."

"I assure you, our law firm values privacy above all else, Ms. Pomeroy."

"Voice mail, please," I stressed.

"Certainly."

I was transferred without another word. At the beep I started talking. "Hello, Miss Walsh. My name is Pepper Pomeroy with Perfect Proposals. Please call me at this number. It is regarding Toby Mallard. Thank you."

Hanging up, I wondered if that message would be enough to get a call back from her. If she was as good as I suspected, she would Google me and find my LinkedIn profile. If she was Toby's love, she would figure out what my call was about. If she wasn't, she just might call me to find out what the heck was going on.

It was a big chance to take. If I spoiled Toby's surprise, he could rightly ask for his money back. I was fully prepared to give him the refund. He had left me no other choice.

Chapter 13

On Saturday I arrived five minutes late to the bridal shop. The parking lot was full and I had to park near the coffee shop and walk. Most likely my sister and her friends had each driven their own car. I recognized my mom's car in the lot as well as Felicity's. Parking beside the shop was at a premium to begin with. I should have called and asked for a ride.

I pulled the door open and saw that the lobby area was empty, which meant that my party was already back in a salon room. Darn, my mom was going to kill me. Then I noticed that it wasn't Theresa at the front desk. It was a guy—a big guy.

"Hello?" I said.

He glanced up. "Hello, how can I help you?" The guy

had an accent like Vidalia. He wore a button-down dress shirt in light blue. It accented his blue eyes and strong features. His hair was blond but cut very short.

"I'm here with the Pomeroy party," I said, and smiled. "I'm a bit late."

"Ah, they are all back in room three. Do you know where it is?"

"Yes," I said. Then I stuck my hand out. "I'm Pepper Pomeroy. Are you Vidalia's brother, Vladimir?"

He stood and I noted that he wore pricey jeans and a brown leather belt. He laughed. "No, no, I am Vidalia's husband, Anton. Vidalia was able to book two appointments this afternoon and asked me to help out so that the front desk would not be empty." He took my hand and gave it a nice shake. "Trust me when I say that Vidalia would never let Vladimir take over the front desk of her mother's bridal shop."

"No?" I shook my head.

"No. He destroys whatever he touches," Anton explained. "Vidalia is quick to forgive him, but she needs to learn to protect herself." He shook his head and sighed. "I do what I can for her but . . ." He let the thought hang.

"Is that why her mother only left Vladimir money and not a portion of the shop?" I bit my bottom lip and tried not to cringe at my own forwardness. The question was probably out of line and he might tell me it was none of my business, but I needed to push if I was to get any answers.

He studied me a moment and I held my breath. "Eva was a smart woman," Anton said, finally. "She loved her son, but she, too, knew what he was like." He shrugged. "It is nice to meet you, Miss Pomeroy. Vidalia has told me a lot about you."

"She has?"

"Certainly, you are the one who found Eva. I wish to thank you for that. I think every day what would have happened had Vidalia walked in on the killer alone."

"Oh, well, we had an appointment."

He walked with me to the end of the hall. "Still, you were here and my wife did not have to see her mother in that state. Number three is the second door on the left."

"Thanks," I said. He seemed like a nice guy. I didn't know what I had thought Vidalia's husband would look like, but it was not the big gentle man I just met. I opened the door and walked in to see the girls oohing and aahing over the bridesmaid's gowns Vidalia held up.

"Color choice is up to the bride," Vidalia was saying.

I gave her a little wave, closed the door, and took a seat next to my mother on the settee.

"Where have you been?" Mom whispered.

"Couldn't find parking," I whispered back as Vidalia continued with her talk about the best colors to complement the bride.

"I'm not sure," Felicity said. "I have been so worried about the gown that I hadn't thought through the colors for the wedding. I really don't want a theme wedding. They feel so silly to me—more like a senior prom than a wedding."

"Good," Vidalia said. "Let me show you the gown and

color I have chosen for your maid of honor. Miss Pepper, come with me."

All eyes in the room looked to me. I shrugged and stood and followed Vidalia out of the room. She walked with me to the small room in the back beside the kitchen. I noted that the back door was no longer boarded closed but instead had a single door-width metal bar fixed across the center.

"I see you changed the door."

"My husband, Anton, did not want to pay the fire marshal's fine."

"Does the bar work? I asked.

"Yes, the back door swings inward. This will stop any invaders, and Theresa now knows she must go out front to smoke. Also it keeps Thad or anyone else from the back entrance. I feel after what happened to my mother that you can never be too careful."

"I agree." I said. She handed me the dress I tried on the other day and pointed to the curtain. I put the dress on and stepped out barefoot. The shoes I wore went well with the skinny jeans I had had on, but looked ridiculous with the gown.

Vidalia fussed over me for a moment. "You need shoes," she said, and went over to the corner and pulled out a pair of pearl-colored, high-heeled sandals. "Put these on."

I slipped them on and was suddenly aware of how much I towered over her.

She stepped back and eyed me. "It is too bad we can do nothing with your hair."

I touched my hair, which I had worn down today. It was humid out and the curls stuck out at least six inches from the sides of my head.

"We will not worry about that detail," she decided out loud. "Come with me."

I teetered on the five-inch heels and tried to keep up with her fast pace. She put her hand on the doorknob and sighed at how far from her I still was.

"Come, come," she said.

I sped up as fast as I could without breaking my ankle. She opened the door and stepped inside.

"Here is the maid of honor." Vidalia waved toward me and I stepped into the room. She helped me up on the dais. When I felt the room go still and everyone's gaze on me, the heat of a blush rushed up my neck and splotched my face. I had my back to the triple mirror.

"Oh, Pepper, you look perfect!" Felicity gushed and stood. She and Mom came over to view me up close at every angle. "Vidalia, you have done it again. My sister has never looked lovelier."

"Thanks, I think," I muttered. Mom gave me the silent stink eye. I bit my inner cheek and sent Mom the "sorry" look. She replied with a narrow-eyed nod.

"It is perfect," Mom said. "I can see where you are going with the entire party. Now you said something about the other girls having different colors?"

"Now that I see their coloring, I know for sure they will have a lighter version of the maid of honor's color. Then, Felicity, I will provide you swatches of the fabrics in the girl's dresses and the pearl fabric from your dress. You take them to your florist and they will create contrasting bouquets for your girls. It will be lovely."

"You are wonderful!" Felicity gave Vidalia a big hug. The saleswoman looked surprised and then delighted as she patted my sister's back.

"Come now," Vidalia said to me. "We'll take off the dress."

We walked out to the hall, leaving my sister and her friends gushing over the dress ideas and colors.

"I met your husband, Anton," I said.

"Yes, I told him that with Mother gone, Theresa needs to step up. Today she is taking her first client in room one. I have learned my lesson. The front desk will never be empty again."

"Are you hiring?" I asked. We stepped into the back room and she unzipped my dress and pushed me to the changing curtain.

"That is the thing. Anton believes we don't need to waste money on another girl. So I have asked him to step in when needed."

I pulled the dress over my head and handed it and the hanger out to her. "I know today is Saturday. What do you do about the rest of the week? Is it easy for him to leave his work?"

"Anton works a few doors down," she said as I got dressed. "He is a cabinetmaker and furniture refinisher, and as co-owner of his shop, he has more freedom. Still, I am certain my plan will work. He will become tired of answering my door, and soon I will be hiring another worker."

"I certainly hope so," I said as I stepped out from behind the curtain. "You are quite good at this, and I think, with our helping you promote the shop, your business will take off."

"It already has," she said with a sly smile. "Theresa is helping a bride who said that Warren Evans had given her mother my name."

"Well, there you go. Another successful small business supported by Warren." I went to fist bump her, but she gave me the strangest look and I let my hand fall down.

"We will go back now and get the other bridesmaids measurements and dress styles."

"Right," I said, and followed her. Checking my phone, I noted that Toby had called. I made a face. I was going to have to talk to him sooner than I had hoped. It was not going to be a fun conversation.

Chapter 14

"Perfect Proposals, how can I help you?"

"Hi, Pepper." Detective Murphy's rumbly voice came through my phone speaker. I was at home looking through five or six rental ads that Mitzy, my Realtor, had sent me via an online portal. When the phone rang, I had answered it on speaker.

"Oh, hi, Detective Murphy," I said, dragging my eyes from a quiet little bungalow in Des Plaines. "How are you? Has there been a break in the case?"

"No break, but . . ."

Oh boy, hesitation was never good. I picked up my phone, switched off the speaker, and sat back in my office chair. "Please tell me you didn't arrest someone I love."

"No, no, the case is still being investigated, although we are close to figuring it out."

"How close?" I asked, drawing my eyebrows together.

"There is a person of interest we are calling in first thing Monday morning."

"Cool, anyone I know?"

"I doubt it."

"Then what can I do for you, Detective?"

"I, um, told my daughter about you."

"You did? Oh, that's sweet. Wait . . . what did you say about me?"

"I told her about your deadbeat boyfriend and how you recently told him to take a hike."

"And?"

"And that you said you wish you had told him to leave years ago."

"I see." I pursed my lips and had a bad feeling this wasn't going the way he had hoped. "What did she say?"

"She said, good for you and she hopes you are happy."

"I am happy."

"That's what I said."

"Oh, don't tell me you told her she should do the same thing!" I felt the horror rise up from my stomach.

"I may have mentioned something like that," he admitted, and sounded so full of regret.

"Oh, Detective Murphy, I told you not to do that. What were you thinking?"

"I was thinking it was a great conversation to have. You know, telling her how you reminded me of her and all."

"While that's very flattering, I'm not so sure she'd appreciate you telling her that her boyfriend is as bad as Bobby."

"I figured that out a bit too late." He sighed. "Now what do I do?"

I ran my hands over my face and brushed the hair out of my eyes. "When did you talk to her?"

"This morning."

I shook my head and my mouth became a single thin line. "I would give her a couple of days before I called again."

"What do I say?"

"You apologize." I heard him wince. "Then you send her flowers and you tell her that you understand that she is an adult and that you know you raised her to make the right choices for her. Then you tell her that you trust her to make those choices on her own and you will never suggest she isn't making good decisions again."

"But she's my kid."

"And she will be your kid for the rest of her life, but that doesn't mean you should be parenting her. Unless she asks for your honest opinion, and even then you need to be careful how you give it."

"Are all girls this complicated?"

"Yes," I said. "If your wife were here, she'd tell you the same thing."

"That's what I was afraid of." He blew out a breath. "Thanks, Pepper."

"You're welcome. Now, as to the investigation, have you thought about Vidalia's brother, Vladimir?"

"What about him?"

"I walked in on Vidalia arguing with her brother over the phone. When I asked about it, she told me that he was upset because he was not given any part of the dress shop when his mother died. He only got cash and didn't think that was fair."

"Family dispute, Pepper," Detective Murphy said in full cop mode. "Besides, it happened after the murder."

"Vidalia's husband, Anton, told me he was glad Vlad got nothing because Vlad is bad news."

"Again, how does that help my investigation?"

"Check out his background. He could have killed his mother because he needed money and hoped to inherit half the shop. Or he could have a record and have gotten away with a few crimes in the past, thus emboldening him to steal things from the shop. When his mother caught him, he killed her."

"Your imagination is far too vivid," Detective Murphy said with a chuckle.

I pouted. "What if I'm right? I'm telling you there is something going on there."

"I'll look into Vladimir's background just like I looked into Thad's."

"You did?"

"Yes, I did, Pepper."

I waited a couple of heartbeats. "And you're not going to tell me what you found."

"This is a police case, Pepper," he said.

"I was thinking about that, too. Did you happen to

keep the coffee cups that Vidalia had in her hands? I'd like to see them."

"Why?"

"They might contain a clue. I could talk to the barista at the coffee shop and find out who drank what. Or—even better—they might have lipstick or fingerprints on them."

"First of all, there is no reason for you to talk to anyone about my case," he chided me. "Secondly, we didn't keep them. There was no reason to do that. Vidalia came into the crime scene carrying them."

"Right."

"Besides, if we had and there was any evidence on them, I couldn't show them to you anyway. You understand that, right?"

"Sure."

"Now, how are you doing? Is that guy . . ." His voice trailed off.

"Bobby?"

"Yes, is Bobby bothering you at all? I know you dated a long time."

"We're good," I said, and glanced at the bar across the street. "In fact, I've been looking for a new apartment. So if you know of anything cute and affordable, I'd be happy for the mention."

He paused.

"What?"

"My mother has a small house in Park Ridge."

"Okay, well, is she looking to rent a room or something?" I winced. "I'm really looking for an apartment."

"See, that's the thing, Mom's ninety-four years old."

"That's a nice thought, but I'm looking for a new place I can really make my own."

"So, you're looking to buy."

"Maybe," I shrugged. "I guess I haven't figured that part out. I'm mostly looking to move away from The Naked Truth."

"What?"

"It's the bar across the street that Bobby practically lives at. That bar is the reason I live here and it's sort of time for me to move on, you know?"

"I get it," he said. "Well, good luck in your search."

"Good luck with your daughter," I said. "Send flowers."

"Yeah, I heard you say that. Bye, Pepper."

"Bye." I hung up and looked out the window. A group of young guys headed into the bar at two in the afternoon. It might be nice to move into a neighborhood without a bar on the corner. That said, did I want to take on a roommate my aunt Betty's age? I wonder how she would react when I wanted to bring Gage home with me.

The idea made me laugh. If I were to move in with Detective Murphy's ninety-four-year-old mom, I might as well put an "Unavailable" sign on my forehead and get some cats . . . a whole lot of cats.

* * *

The next day I stopped by the dress shop to pay the next portion of the bill for my bridesmaid dress. The dresses were custom sewn and not cheap. Thankfully Vidalia had a payment plan that split the cost into four parts. I didn't have Mom's great negotiation skills behind my purchase, but then she wasn't buying my dress.

Luckily the parking lot was emptier and I was able to find a space quickly. I didn't mind walking my payment in because it gave me an excuse to ask Vidalia how the case was going and if she remembered anything more about the day her mother died.

I pulled the door open and discovered a new man at the front desk. He had the same strong Eastern European features as Vidalia and her husband, Anton. "Hello," I said as I stepped up to the desk. The sleuth in me was aware that the door did not slam behind me like it did the first time. I assumed that meant that Vidalia still had the back door secure.

"Hello, how can I help you?" The man had darker hair than Vidalia but his eyes were very similar. He was slight of build and wore a pale pink dress shirt with a deeper pink tie with tiny white polka dots. He stood when I entered.

"I'm Pepper Pomeroy." I stuck out my hand. He shook it firmly.

"Ah, are you the Ms. Pepper who discovered my mother's body and then brought in her family to save our family's bridal business?"

The heat of a blush rushed up my cheeks. "I'm not sure I'd say that I saved your family's business. Your sister is very good at what she does."

"Of course she is." He waved the thought away. "Please sit. I am Vladimir Svetkovska."

I took the chair next to the front desk. "Nice to meet you, Vladimir." He was much younger than I had thought. My guess would be he was ten years younger than Anton and about four years younger than Vidalia.

"Certainly," he said. "What makes an important person such as yourself come into the shop?"

"I'm here to make a partial payment. Vidalia set me up on credit for my maid of honor gown."

"I see," he said. "One moment and I will bring up your account on the computer."

"I'm surprised to see you here," I said.

"You are? Why? This is my family's business."

"Yes, of course, but Vidalia told me you were unhappy with your mother's will. I mean, I know Eva left the shop to your sister and yet here you are." I paused a moment. Okay, so my question was a bit nosey but I had to know. "Look, I know it's none of my business, but since you are here, I assume Vidalia is fixing the oversight and giving you your half of the shop. I mean, she seems like she would do the right thing for you."

Vladimir's face turned a sudden deep purple red and his eyes narrowed. There was a tic in his jaw and I sat back to put some space between us. "No." Vlad said. "Anton would never let her do anything like that. I am here as a temporary assistant. Even then I doubt he will let her keep me here for long."

"Wow, sorry," I murmured to soothe his visible anger. "I had no idea or I would not have brought it up."

"My sister and her husband are greedy. They think

172

because I have had a few unsuccessful attempts at starting my own business that I am no good. This is madness. New start-ups fail all the time. This is not my fault. First the location was terrible. Then the bankers they don't allow me time to get momentum going. They do not give me extra money to put out enough advertising." He took a deep breath. "Then my partner skimmed from the top. His wife would come in and take money right out of the drawer, and when I told him that she needed to stop, he would do nothing about it. None of this is my fault."

He turned to the computer and tapped on the keys. "It is ridiculous that my sister does not understand this. She has our mother's business. She had never dealt with a start-up." He looked at me. "You payment is two hundred and fifty dollars."

I pulled out my checkbook and filled out a check as he continued with his rant.

"I could make her and Anton millionaires. But they do not offer me as much as a nickel for my next idea. So here I am working for peanuts as a temporary assistant at a shop that is rightfully half mine."

Ripping off the check, I said, "Perhaps they only wish to motivate you. You could do it without them and show them how wrong they are. Can you imagine how good you'll feel when they see that you're a huge success?"

He took my check and logged it into the computer and printed off my receipt. "No, they wish to keep me from my success. They have refused to be my reference, and worse, they have refused to cosign my next loan."

"It is because you have already lost Vidalia a lot of money," Theresa said as she came around the corner. "And you are lazy. Everyone knows this. I heard Vidalia's friends tell her not to even think about loaning you money. Even here, I have to do your job as well as mine." She gathered up some cups from the waiting area and placed them on a tray. "You know you must never allow dishes to remain in this area."

"I was getting to it."

Theresa snorted. "I'm sure you were." She walked out with her back straight and her nose in the air. I found her such an odd girl. She never even acknowledged me in the room.

"It was nice to meet you, Vladimir," I said as I picked up my receipt and stood. "I wish you luck on your next venture."

"I don't need luck. I will make a lot of money and show them all," he shouted over his shoulder so that Theresa would hear him in the back room. Then he turned to me. "Would you wish to invest with me?"

I smiled awkwardly. "No, I've got a new business and am cash poor. It's why I'm making payments on my dress. I'm sure you understand."

"I do and I'm certain no one calls you lazy."

"Good-bye, Vladimir," I said, and headed out the door. I could not get out of there fast enough. Between Vlad and Theresa, the atmosphere was so uncomfortable I felt sorry for Vidalia. These two alone could drive potential customers away.

"It is because you have already lost Vidalia a lot of money," Theresa said as she came around the corner. "And you are lazy. Everyone knows this. I heard Vidalia's friends tell her not to even think about loaning you money. Even here, I have to do your job as well as mine." She gathered up some cups from the waiting area and placed them on a tray. "You know you must never allow dishes to remain in this area."

"I was getting to it."

Theresa snorted. "I'm sure you were." She walked out with her back straight and her nose in the air. I found her such an odd girl. She never even acknowledged me in the room.

"It was nice to meet you, Vladimir," I said as I picked up my receipt and stood. "I wish you luck on your next venture."

"I don't need luck. I will make a lot of money and show hem all," he shouted over his shoulder so that Theresa ould hear him in the back room. Then he turned to me. Vould you wish to invest with me?"

I smiled awkwardly. "No, I've got a new business and cash poor. It's why I'm making payments on my dress. sure you understand."

do and I'm certain no one calls you lazy."

ood-bye, Vladimir," I said, and headed out the door d not get out of there fast enough. Between V heresa, the atmosphere was so uncomfortabl or Vidalia. These two alone could drive ers away.

a payment plan that split the cost into four parts. I didn't have Mom's great negotiation skills behind my purchase, but then she wasn't buying my dress.

Luckily the parking lot was emptier and I was able to find a space quickly. I didn't mind walking my payment in because it gave me an excuse to ask Vidalia how the case was going and if she remembered anything more about the day her mother died.

I pulled the door open and discovered a new man at the front desk. He had the same strong Eastern European features as Vidalia and her husband, Anton. "Hello," I said as I stepped up to the desk. The sleuth in me was aware that the door did not slam behind me like it did the first time. I assumed that meant that Vidalia still had the back door secure.

"Hello, how can I help you?" The man had darker hair than Vidalia but his eyes were very similar. He was slight of build and wore a pale pink dress shirt with a deeper pink tie with tiny white polka dots. He stood when I entered.

"I'm Pepper Pomeroy." I stuck out my hand. He shook it firmly.

"Ah, are you the Ms. Pepper who discovered my mother's body and then brought in her family to save our family's bridal business?"

The heat of a blush rushed up my cheeks. "I'm not sure I'd say that I saved your family's business. Your sister is very good at what she does."

"Of course she is." He waved the thought away. "Please sit. I am Vladimir Svetkovska."

I took the chair next to the front desk. "Nice to meet you, Vladimir." He was much younger than I had thought. My guess would be he was ten years younger than Anton and about four years younger than Vidalia.

"Certainly," he said. "What makes an important person such as yourself come into the shop?"

"I'm here to make a partial payment. Vidalia set me up on credit for my maid of honor gown."

"I see," he said. "One moment and I will bring up your account on the computer."

"I'm surprised to see you here," I said.

"You are? Why? This is my family's business."

"Yes, of course, but Vidalia told me you were unhappy with your mother's will. I mean, I know Eva left the shop to your sister and yet here you are." I paused a moment. Okay, so my question was a bit nosey but I had to know. "Look, I know it's none of my business, but since you are here, I assume Vidalia is fixing the oversight and giving you your half of the shop. I mean, she seems like she would do the right thing for you."

Vladimir's face turned a sudden deep purple red and his eyes narrowed. There was a tic in his jaw and I sat back to put some space between us. "No." Vlad said. "Anton would never let her do anything like that. I am here as a temporary assistant. Even then I doubt he will let her keep me here for long."

"Wow, sorry," I murmured to soothe his visible anger. "I had no idea or I would not have brought it up."

"My sister and her husband are greedy. They think

because I have had a few unsuccessful attempts at starting my own business that I am no good. This is madness. New start-ups fail all the time. This is not my fault. First the location was terrible. Then the bankers they don't allow me time to get momentum going. They do not give me extra money to put out enough advertising." He took a deep breath. "Then my partner skimmed from the top. His wife would come in and take money right out of the drawer, and when I told him that she needed to stop, he would do nothing about it. None of this is my fault."

He turned to the computer and tapped on the keys. " is ridiculous that my sister does not understand this. has our mother's business. She had never dealt w start-up." He looked at me. "You payment is two hu and fifty dollars."

I pulled out my checkbook and filled out a he continued with his rant.

"I could make her and Anton millionaire do not offer me as much as a nickel for my here I am working for peanuts as a tempora a shop that is rightfully half mine."

Ripping off the check, I said, "Perhaps to motivate you. You could do it withou them how wrong they are. Can you i you'll feel when they see that you're

He took my check and logged it i printed off my receipt. "No, they v my success. They have refused to orse, they have refused to cosi

Chapter 15

"Thank you for meeting me for coffee," I said to Laura. "I know how very busy you must be, being a partner in such an exclusive firm."

We sat together in a trendy coffee bar downtown. It had been two weeks since Toby had contacted me. I had finally gotten her to say yes to meeting me, with the promise of reservations at the coffee bar that had just opened. I still had connections from my event-planning days. The reservations alone had cost me fifty dollars since I had to bribe my way into the place.

"I have no idea why you are so interested in seeing me that you are spending twenty dollars for a cup for coffee, but you have my full attention." Laura was lovely with dark hair and porcelain skin, and she was wearing a navy blue Armani suite with a silk blouse.

"I need to know more about you and Toby Mallard," I said, cutting straight to the chase.

"Who?"

"Toby Mallard," I repeated suddenly, sure that my instincts were correct as usual and now not only would I have to give back the ten grand Toby gave me, but I'd be out the fifty dollars plus the twenty bucks two cups of coffee cost me for this meeting. "He said you and he were dating."

"I'm sorry. Do you have a picture of him? I've recently divorced and have been on a silly dating site. Men like to give themselves strange names like 'I'm the One' or 'Fish 410.' "

I frowned. "No, I don't have a photo. But the fact that you need a photo answers all my questions."

"Well, that's something, I suppose," she said. "I hope it was worth your time and money. The coffee is really good here, but I'm pretty certain I won't be back unless it's on a client's dime." She sent me a small smile. "Out of curiosity, why are you asking? Are you a private investigator or something? Does he have a jealous wife I should be worried about?"

I laughed and took out my card. "I'm a proposal planner."

"Perfect Proposals," she read, and looked up at me, her eyebrows drawn together. "I don't understand."

"Toby Mallard paid me ten thousand dollars to plan a large and over-the-top wedding proposal event."

"A wedding proposal event?"

"Yes." I nodded, my lips pursed.

"What does that have to do with me?" She handed me back my card.

"He said you were the love of his life and he hired me to plan—"

"An event proposal to me?"

"Yes."

She frowned deeply. "This Toby wants to ask me to marry him?"

"To the tune of a ten grand retainer, to start."

"That's crazy." Her hands shook as she put down her coffee cup. The cups were mere thimbles, really. You came to the coffee shop for the atmosphere and the cache that you had been. The coffee was Kopi Luwak coffee. The rare kind where they found the beans in lemur poop or more specifically civet poop, then washed and roasted them for a distinct smooth, nutty flavor. "Is he stalking me?" she asked. "Should I be concerned? Do I need a restraining order?"

"I don't think so." I patted her hand in an attempt to comfort her. "He seems to be a bit distracted. All he had was a photo of you on his phone. Apparently you run marathons?"

"Yes."

"He has a picture of you finishing the Chicago marathon."

"The one in the *Tribune*?"

"If that's the one on your Facebook profile, than yes," I answered. "That was my first real clue that things were a bit off. The only picture he had of you was that one. He put me on retainer and asked me to set up a wedding proposal, but he couldn't tell me anything about you except that you were a lawyer and a runner. You see, I specialize in getting to know the potential bride and both families, and I plan the event based on what the woman likes to do or what the couple did while dating. Toby could give me none of that information."

"So you came straight to the source."

"I did." I sipped the coffee which was very good if you didn't think about the fact that the bean had been pooped out of an animal in Bali.

"What if I had been dating him? Would that have given his proposal away?"

"I would have come up with a cover story." I shrugged. "It was a chance I had to take. I couldn't find out anything about your family or friends. Your Facebook page is blocked. And your LinkedIn profile was all work."

"Now I'm curious. What does this Toby look like?"

"He is kind of a cross between Columbo and George Clooney."

"Well, that certainly sounds interesting."

I raised a corner of my mouth in a wry grin. "It is." I stood and she stood. "Thank you for your time." We shook hands and she tried to give me back my card. "No," I said, and waved it off. "Keep it. You never know if you or a friend might need a hand planning the perfect proposal . . . or dodging one."

She laughed. "Indeed. Thank you. I'll watch out for this

Toby guy. If I feel he's stalking me, I'm getting a restraining order."

"Be my guest," I said. "At this point I can't guarantee he isn't crazy."

"Thanks," she said.

"You're welcome," I said. "I feel that vetting the clients that don't sound right is an important part of my job."

"I'm happy to help."

She might have been happy, but I wasn't. After we left, I went back to Old Blue, sighed at the twenty-dollar parking fee, and decided that I would simply bill Toby for expenses plus my time and the effort it took to figure out he was a nut case. After all, that's what retainers are for, right?

I dialed Gage and put him on speakerphone. Ever since Chicago banned cell phones while driving, I had been especially careful to use my car speakers. Thank goodness for Bluetooth technology.

"Prop warehouse, this is Gage speaking, how can I help you today?"

"Hi, Gage, it's Pepper."

"Hey, Pepper, how you doing?"

I laughed at his imitation of the character Joey from *Friends*. Last time we met we had had this conversation about Chicagoans and how often they said that to each other. "Better now that I'm talking to you."

"What's up?"

"I finally got to talk to that Toby guy's girl. You know, the one he wants to propose to but could tell me nothing about."

"Right. How'd that work out?"

"Not so good. It turns out she doesn't even know who he is."

"Oh, that's not good."

"Right? I figured I'd ask a guy if he had any idea why another guy would do this."

"Try to propose to a girl he's never met?" Gage asked. "Pretty much sounds like a guy who gets what he wants with little effort."

"Hmmm, he did say he pays his people to make him money."

"Well, there you go. My advice is that you're going to have to tell him from a strictly female perspective that that doesn't work. No matter how rich the guy is."

"Okay, strictly speaking, there are some women out there who would marry a guy she doesn't know just for his money. Why do you think they had that television show about marrying a millionaire?"

"That's laziness on both their parts, if you ask me. They deserve each other."

"I don't think that's what he wants," I said as I drove down Interstate 90. "I think he picked Laura because she is smart, beautiful, and successful in her own right."

"Call him, Pepper," Gage said. "He has to know that if she is the kind of woman he wants, he needs to go out there and get her himself."

"Sounds like you have some experience in that area," I teased.

"I'm trying," he said, sincerity in his voice. "When are

we going out again, Pepper? It's been a couple of weeks. It was great fun going through the estate I bought for the warehouse, but I wouldn't really call that a date."

I winced. "I've been a little crazy what with Mary's proposal, Alexander's proposal, and Felicity's wedding stuff."

"Not to mention investigating that murder."

"I'm a proposal planner not an investigator," I reminded him. "Besides, it's weird to try to date you with Bobby next door in that bar."

"How's the hunt for a new place going?" he asked. "All these excuses can leave a guy thinking he might be rejected at any moment."

"I have a lead on a place that might be nice," I improvised. "The thing is that there might be a ninety-four-year-old-woman involved."

"In my experience, older women are pretty tolerant," he said. "Who is it?"

"It's Detective Murphy's mother. He said she has a place in Park Ridge."

"It can't hurt to go look," Gage said. "Want me to come with you?"

"No, thanks," I said. "I'm going to go see Toby in person. I don't really have the time to indulge Detective Murphy. I'll just keep looking online."

"And our date?"

"You are persistent."

"Very," he said, and I could hear the smile in his voice. "Resistance is futile."

"Oh, for goodness sake." I rolled my eyes at the old

Star Trek quote. "Fine, I do want to see you. It's been too long."

"Let's go out Saturday at nine," he said. "I'll make reservations. You wear something sexy and we'll see what happens from there."

I did so love the low timbre in his voice when he gave hints of more to come. It made my heart race and my knees go weak. "I'll be there," I said.

"Wonderful."

I hung up the phone feeling good. I've known Gage my whole life. For most of it all I really knew was that he was Bobby's best friend and deserved far better than the way Bobby treated him. But then again, so did I.

I remember being shocked when Gage first approached me. I hadn't seen it coming. But now looking back, all the signs were there. Gage had been Bobby's friend for so long simply to stay close to me.

There was something very romantic about the whole thing. I sighed and turned off the highway. From that good conversation to the next bad conversation, it was time to see Toby and confront him about Laura.

Chapter 16

I met Toby at a small business café. They had a few around the area. It was basically a large open and airy room. There were couches and chairs and even a few desks strewn about. There were also tables for teams of up to six to sit and work. The atmosphere was one of hushed quiet with free Wi-Fi. They had a bar on the right where you could order coffee, tea, pastries, and fruit. The room had all the amenities of a corporate break room. And like a corporation break room, there were two refrigerators side by side to hold your lunch. In the back were three glass-walled conference room spaces for meetings.

It was the twenty-first-century version of a home office. It gave people who worked from home or people who started their own business a place to come when they needed to get out of the house or meet with clients.

I had called and booked the smallest conference room in the back. It was more expensive than booking a conference room at the local library, but this time I wanted to ensure that Toby didn't have any movies or books to distract him from our conversation.

I arrived and set up my laptop. The café had a printing service that cost five cents per page, but I already had my own printer and had preprinted everything I needed. Next I went and ordered a pot of coffee, hot water, and assorted teas, along with a small pastry tray. After all, the bill was on Toby.

He was prompt.

"Hello, Toby, thanks for meeting me on such short notice. Please have a seat." I closed the door behind him. "Can I offer you coffee or tea?" I waved at the tray on the table. "Perhaps a muffin?"

Toby looked as if he had just gotten out of bed, thrown on clothes he'd left on the floor, and come on down. He had a bit of a five-o'clock shadow going that was gray and didn't look too bad on him. In fact it sort of toughened up the roundness of his face. He smelled good.

"Coffee's fine," he said, and sat down. "Black." I poured him a cup and we sat in what felt to me like awkward silence, but I'm not sure he noticed.

"I spoke to Laura," I said.

"How did you get her to meet with you?" he asked, his thick eyebrows drawn together.

"I have my ways. Besides, you'll see it in your itemized bill," I said briskly. "You have not been honest with me, Toby, and I don't like dishonest clients." I gave him my best version of a mother's stare. You know the one. Where she lets you know in no uncertain terms that you have been caught in a lie.

He merely shrugged and poured sugar into his coffee even though he'd asked for it black.

"Toby, Laura doesn't even know who you are. How did you decide you were going to propose to her?"

"I saw her at a charity event I attended last month," he said. "Then I searched for her online and ran a background check." He sipped his coffee and reached for a slice of pound cake. "I'm at the point in my life where marriage is the next logical step. Then in a year or two I should have children. Mid to late thirties is the optimal time for men to marry and have children. Laura is twenty-nine years old. She only has a year or two of her prime childbearing years left, and I figured she was ready to do the same."

"You wanted to propose to her because you are ready and you believe she is ready to build a family based on your ages?"

"Oh, there is more than that. There is family health history and risk of disease, et cetera. I've taken it all into account, as I did when I hired you."

"Toby, love doesn't work that way." I folded my hands on the tabletop.

"Certainly it does," he said. "I have read the research

that nine times out of ten a woman feels her biological clock ticking and begins her search for her ideal mate. That ideal is a man in his mid to late thirties with enough money to support her and her children in a manner she is either used to or wishes to get used to. A man, on the other hand, looks for a woman who is pretty enough to show his friends that he has the monetary stature to obtain her—thus the term 'trophy wife.' Also, I prefer a woman who is smart enough to not bore me to tears. Beyond that there are some studies that suggest intelligence is genetically handed down by the female of the species. Laura worked on all fronts. Did you tell her what I was proposing?"

I bit my bottom lip. "Surprise is a big factor in creating a perfect proposal," I said. "It made this meeting with Laura difficult. I began by asking her if she was dating you."

"I see." He sipped coffee. "When she said she was not?"

"I told her who I was, who you were, and what you wanted."

He took a bite of his cake and thoughtfully washed it down with more coffee. "Interesting. What was her reaction?"

"She asked if she needed to take a restraining order out on you." That was pretty cut and dry as far as I was concerned. You had to be careful with certain men. They didn't always understand what *no* means. Especially if you said it nicely.

"Huh."

"In the interest of business, I have an itemized bill for my time and services necessary to discover that you are not actually dating Laura and she is not actually interested in a proposal no matter how grand." I slipped him the bill, which I bumped up to three thousand dollars in hopes that he realized how expensive this entire fruitless endeavor was. "I have cut you a check for the remainder of your retainer." I handed him the seven thousand dollars that I hated to part with but couldn't keep, in all fairness to the poor slob.

"Look," I said. "You seem like a very smart guy, so I will tell you what I know from a female perspective. Women want to be wooed. We want the dates, the drinks, and the fun times. We want to fall in love with a man who gets to know us. We want him to know what we like, what we don't like. We want him to pay attention to the details." Gage came to my mind. He knew how I took my coffee. He knew I would love to go through the estate sale finds he bought and see what treasures we could discover. He brought me flowers.

There was a long pause while Toby seemed to process this information. "So courtship is more important to a woman than money and the ability to give her children and care for them at a higher social economic status."

I sighed. "It's not that the ability to care for our children isn't important." I thought of Bobby and was suddenly glad I dodged that bullet. "Courtship is an important part of the entire process. Almost every living creature has a courtship period. Women need that. Their families need it, too."

Toby's expression was one of thoughtful confusion.

I felt sorry for the guy. This might be the first time in his life he'd come up against something he didn't understand. "Look, I have a proposal event tomorrow," I said. "Why don't you come and watch what happens. It will help you understand how important relationships are to the couple getting married and to their combined families."

"I don't have to worry about my family," he said. "My mother is in a nursing home and my father is dead. I'm an only child."

That explained a lot, if you asked me. "But the woman you eventually marry will have a family. Please come and see it for yourself firsthand."

"Fine," he said, and finished his cake and coffee. "What time and where?"

"It's at the DuPage Airport in West Chicago at ten A.M. Arrive fifteen minutes early and look for me. I'll be tweaking last-minute details, so just look for me wearing a headset. Whatever you do, do not tell anyone why you are there other than to meet me. The event is a surprise and since you don't know anyone, you don't want to give it away to the wrong person. Okay?"

"All right," he said and stood. "Good day, Ms. Pomeroy."

I stood as well and shook his hand. "I'm sorry it didn't work out for you."

"I've come to expect these things in business," he said as he folded up my invoice and pocketed my check. "Good day."

I sat down and watched him go. All in all he took it well. He really wasn't a bad sort of guy, just a little clueless. I poured myself some coffee and put a blueberry pastry on a plate. I still had fifteen minutes left in the meeting room, so I used it to work.

Everything was in order for Alexander's engagement. Mary's was coming along nicely. But after that the well had run a little dry. It was time to drum up a little business. I did it by creating a Pinterest board with other people's fantastical proposals. There was the pro cheerleader whose boyfriend proposed with a flash mob at halftime. Then there was the couple who got engaged at the top of Mount Everest—which was not a proposal event I would ever plan no matter how much they paid me. I was not that happy when faced with a lack of oxygen.

Pinterest was perfect for gaining ideas as well. Girls tended to pin their dream weddings. I liked to see how they put things together and envision how I would have used that information to create a perfect proposal.

Then I paid for a Craigslist ad to let the public know that Perfect Proposals was the best proposal planning company out there. In Chicago it was the only such company. I left my work phone number on the advertisement along with my e-mail. Hopefully Cesar's video of the jumping couple would draw coverage from the five-o'clock news as a human interest story. That kind of publicity was something you simply couldn't buy.

I packed up, careful to ensure that the remainder of the pastries were carefully wrapped. I'd drop them by Gage's office. A woman who lived alone did not need a half-dozen baked goods sitting in her kitchen. Better to hand them off to a warehouse full of men who would devour them in an instant.

My phone rang when I got into my car. "Perfect Proposals, this is Pepper Pomeroy. How can I help you?"

"Hey, Pepper." Detective Murphy's voice came over the phone. "Are you driving?"

"No, not yet."

"Good," he said, and I rolled my eyes. "Listen, we found almost all of the items stolen from Eva's bridal shop."

"Oh, that's wonderful. Vidalia will be so happy. She was telling me that most were one-of-a-kind pieces. How and where did you find them?"

"They were put up for sale online," he said.

"How were you able to find the dresses? How do you know they were Vidalia's?," I asked. "Have you tracked down the owner of the site yet?"

"Slow down," he cautioned. "We have divisions for online theft and fraud. Their whole job is to track down stolen goods. They were able to confirm that the dresses were the same one-of-a-kind sample dresses that Vidalia listed."

"So was it the thief who listed them online? I mean, that would be too easy, right?"

"You would be surprised how often that happens—where the thief lists stolen goods online. They aren't the brightest people sometimes. In this case, it wasn't the thief. The posters ran an online service. They claim they didn't know the goods were stolen. They got a box in the mail with the items and a substantial wad of cash."

"And no return address on the box . . ."

"That's correct," he said. "Listen, I spoke with my Mom," he said, and I felt my heart go straight to the bottom of my stomach. "She said she would love a renter. Why don't you go down and let her give you a tour. You don't have to rent. I promise. But it would make her day to meet you."

"Fine," I said with a sigh. "What's the address?" I wrote down what he rattled off.

"I told her you'd stop by this afternoon," he said. "Will three P.M. work?"

"Really?" I could not believe he did this to me. It was something my parents would do. I know he said I reminded him of his daughter, but that nostalgia might have gone a little too far. "Detective Murphy—"

"I have more information on the case," he interrupted.

"Okay . . ."

"Will you be there at three?"

"This feels a bit like blackmail," I said. "But yes, I'll be there at three. Now, tell me what else you know about the case."

"We've brought in Theresa's boyfriend, Thad. Turns out he has a history of theft and burglary."

"Wow," was all I could say. "I knew there was something not right about the kid, but he seems kind of young and scrawny to have killed Eva. Are you charging him?"

"When we showed him that we found the dresses online, he admitted to the theft," Detective Murphy said.

"So Thad stole the dresses. Why?"

"He said he needed the dress money to pay off his bookie."

"No, I mean why did he kill Eva? He doesn't seem the murderous type. What was his motive?

"It was a crime of convenience. Thad swears Eva was alive when he stole the goods, but we have his prints from the back door."

"You have my prints on the back door," I pointed out.

"Yes, but we're pretty sure he was headed out the back door with the samples when Eva caught him. Most likely, she was the one to grab the knife and go after him to try to stop him. They fought and he stabbed Eva. She died and he panicked, wiped off the handle of the knife with one of the stolen pieces, and then took off down the alley. It fits the timeline."

"He ruined his entire life—not to mention Eva's—all to pay off his bookie."

"He said if he had not paid off the bookie he was a walking dead man."

I frowned. "What bookie lets a boy that age make a bet that big?"

"Someone with enough money down to make it seem like a sure thing," Detective Murphy said. "We brought Theresa in as well."

"Oh, no! Not Theresa. I mean, she seems odd to me, but I can't imagine she could ever murder anyone."

"Theresa told us that she had gone to Eva out of desperation to ask for a loan for Thad, but Eva refused. She gave Theresa a lecture about what kind of boy she should be dating."

"Let me guess, Theresa was so upset she went home sick."

"Yes," the detective said. "That's what she says, anyway. And both her next door neighbor and her mother corroborated her alibi. Now, aren't you glad you said you would go see my mom's place?"

"Yes," I said. "It sounds like you have the case solved."

"The bad guys are under wraps. Thanks for your help."

"I didn't do much."

"You told me about Thad and you're going to see my mom. It'll make her day, Pepper. Don't be late."

"Right."

"She makes the best chocolate chip cookies," he teased.

"I'll be prompt."

"Good girl."

Chapter 17

Mrs. Murphy lived in Park Ridge, a neighborhood of Chicago bungalows and two-story Federalist-style brick homes. The trees that lined the streets were large and the garages sat back behind the homes. It reminded me of my mom and dad's neighborhood. I had to wonder how cool it was going to be to live in a sleepy suburb with a bunch of elderly folks. I was young and vibrant and thirty, for goodness sakes. All my old coworkers lived in the city in artsy neighborhoods near bars and theaters and the lake and such.

Two doors down from the address Detective Murphy had given me, a short, bald, heavy-set man wearing a white wife-beater T-shirt and shorts got up to check out Old Blue as I drove by. I waved. He scowled.

Swallowing hard, I pulled up in front of the brick bungalow. It was one-story with six wide steps that led to a front porch the width of the home. There was a fence surrounding the yard. A flat piece of lawn was split in half by an older cement sidewalk. The weather in Chicago crumbled the best cement with its extreme cold, snow, deep freezes, and thaws. This one was no exception.

The roof looked new and the windows were polished to a soft sheen. There were pots of colorful flowers lining the stairs and hanging from the eaves of the porch. I noticed the front curtain move.

It was go time. I didn't have to rent here. All I needed to do was to meet the old lady, eat a cookie or two, and see the house. Easy, peasy.

I got out, hitched my purse up over my shoulder, and locked Old Blue's doors with my key. The boat of an Oldsmobile didn't have automatic locks, which meant I had to remember to lock the doors myself or take the chance of losing my only means of transportation. Since I had just given Toby seven grand back, I needed to ensure no one would steal my car.

A quick look around had me noticing that front curtains moved in nearly every house in the neighborhood. Maybe I didn't need to lock my car. After all, I knew that many retired cops lived in this area. Plus, a lot of older people spent time at their front window looking for signs of anything out of the ordinary. Such as a tall, skinny redhead pulling up to Mrs. Murphy's in a big blue Oldsmobile.

The front gate opened without a squeak. The steps were

clean and the porch floor was painted gray while the ceiling was painted blue. I knocked.

"Coming," said a voice from within. The wooden door with three small triangles of glass cut into it was pulled open. Mrs. Murphy was a tiny thing, no taller than my shoulder. She wore blue jeans and a T-shirt in a peacock blue color that set off her tightly curled orange hair. Blue eyes smiled back at me as she opened the storm door. "Well, hello, you must be Miss Pomeroy."

"It's Pepper," I said and smiled.

"How wonderful, please come in, come in, we've given the neighbors enough of a show for now."

I walked into the front room. The old plaster walls from the 1920s were lovingly preserved and painted a soft blue. Under my feet was a very cushy carpet in what I would guess was a high-end wool. The curtains were blue silk and looked to be right out of a modern showroom. She had an overstuffed couch in darker blue and a pair of wing chairs covered in a blue and white toile pattern. The only thing about the room that reminded me of my grandmother was the tufted round pillows on the couch.

"I'll give you the nickel tour. This is the living room," she said. "That opens to the dining room." The two were separated by a half wall. Both rooms had white wood trim. The dining room had stained glass windows between built-in bookshelves with built-in china cabinets in both corners.

"Those are lovely, are they original?"

"Yes, my Charlie had them put in when he built the house," she said. "It was 1929 and he'd seen some of the prairie homes and wanted to add his own version to this house. Back here is the kitchen."

"You home is very much like my parents' home," I said.

"It was the style of the time," she said. "Much like split levels of the seventies and eighties and the McMansions of the turn of the century."

Her kitchen was nothing like my parents' kitchen, though, with their old oak cabinets that went clear to the ceiling. This kitchen had to have been redone recently. The cabinets were all white with granite countertops, an island, and stainless steel appliances. The flooring looked like bamboo, polished to a high sheen.

"Wow."

"I know, isn't it gorgeous? I had it redone because I wanted to sell, but then after seeing it, I simply couldn't bring myself to do the deed."

The scent of coffee filled the air, and fresh, gooey looking and, I assume, homemade chocolate chip cookies sat on the table. I nearly reached out and snitched one as she kept walking. But instead I minded my manners. "Through here is the single bathroom. It used to sit between two bedrooms, but I had the whole thing turned into a master suite. You see the bathroom has access here for guests, but there is a door in the side for bedroom access. The architect made the bathroom much larger and then used the remainder of the old bedroom space to create a walk-in closet.

I had to restrain myself from whistling "Wow!" again; the floors were bamboo throughout. The bathroom was three times the size of my current one, with two pedestal sinks, a giant claw-footed tub, a shower, and a separate little room for the toilet. The walls were covered with rectangular blue glass tiles that gave the feel of the sea. Inside the walk-in closet was a window to let in natural light and a built-in vanity with bulb lights surrounding a magnifier mirror. The rest of the walls were built-in cedar California closets.

"This is simply gorgeous," I said, and ran my hand along the soft-scented cedar. "If you took out the second bedroom, then I assume the rental is the third bedroom that opens to the living room?"

She laughed at my confusion. "Oh, no, dear, the entire house is the rental. I'm moving to Florida with my girl-friends. It's why I had the place fixed up and was going to sell it. But between my son Brian's sadness at the loss of his childhood home and my love for all the fine details, I simply couldn't do it. When Brian heard you were looking to rent, I hoped I'd found a responsible renter."

"Oh," I said, and felt the roundness of my mouth at the surprise. "This entire place is for rent?"

"Yes, silly, what did you think? My son wanted you to live with an old woman and be her nanny?" She laughed and it was a trill that lifted the heart.

"Now, there is another bedroom located in the finished basement, along with a smaller sitting area and bath. If you ever feel the need for a roommate to help pay the rent, you can rent it out. I trust you to find someone nice to live down there."

"Okay." That had me worried. How expensive was this place?

"Come on, let's take a quick peek before we have some coffee and cookies and get to know each other properly."

Her quick peek took me from the kitchen door to a small porch on the back that served as a shared foyer. Off the right side of the porch was a door to the basement. The downstairs revealed a shared laundry room with built-in shelves, front-loading washer and dryer, and a built-in ironing board—not that I ironed much. That's what dry cleaners were for. Beyond that was indeed a small one-bedroom suite complete with shower and toilet, sitting area with light from the glass-blocked windows, and a twelve-by-twelve-foot bedroom.

The place was ideal. I pinched myself on the way up the stairs. All I could do now was pray I could afford the rent or find someone who could live in the basement and help out.

"Have a seat, dear." She pointed to her kitchen table, then poured coffee into a thermal carafe. "Help yourself."

I took a cookie—okay, two cookies—and put them on a plate in front of me. "Thank you for the tour. The house is fantastic."

"Better than you thought, isn't it?" She raised an eyebrow at me, poured coffee into my cup, and sat down. "Brian was concerned about my renting. He didn't want me to leave the house in the hands of a Realtor to pick the renters and to ensure they pay. Renting is hard because there are people who will squat. That is to say pay a few months and then stop paying. Then it takes forever to get them out of the house."

"I'm sure that wouldn't happen to you. Your son is a police officer."

"So were his father and his grandfather," she said. "It's why he's so paranoid." She added cream and sugar to her coffee.

I had already put in my customary amount of cream and was done with an entire cookie, which, by the way, was fantastic. "Do you give away your cookie recipe? These are awesome."

"Oh, sure," she said with a wave of her hand. "I make the Toll House recipe on the back of the bag. Always have."

"Huh," I said. "They don't taste this way when I make them."

"I suppose I've been making them longer, is all. Now, my son tells me that you have started your own business recently."

"Yes, Perfect Proposals," I said. "I'm an event planner, and when my sister's fiancé asked me to help plan the ideal proposal, it turned out so well that he financed my business."

"Are you making a profit?"

"Yes, actually, I am. That said, I am in start-up mode so I have to tell you that while I love, love, love the house, I'm afraid I might not be able to afford to rent it."

"I see," she said, and sipped her coffee. "Have you lived in the area your entire life?"

"Yes, I have. My parents don't live too far from here. My sister lives downtown. My aunt Betty lives near Naperville."

"Then you know how much it floods."

"Yes," I said, and snagged two more cookies.

"And sewers back up and then if it gets too cold in the winter, pipes can freeze."

"I know. My parents had trouble with ice dams one year where the cold and ice built up under their eaves and caused the roof to leak."

"I bet you know people who work on that kind of thing. You know, plumbers and roofers and flood restoration."

"I sure do. My father is a plumber." I swallowed my third cookie and tilted my head as I reached for my coffee. "Why do you ask?"

"What is your rent right now?"

"Twelve hundred, plus utilities."

"I'd be willing to let you rent for a thousand a month as long as you took care of anything that might come up."

"Are you kidding me?"

"Think carefully on it," she said, and cupped her coffee mug in her fingers. "It's an old house. You would have to keep on top of things like leaks and pipes and sewer backups. There won't be a property manager to come and fix things for you. That would be your responsibility."

"Wow, a thousand a month."

"Brian would stop by once a month or so and check on the place." She held up her hand before I could say anything. "No, he won't be going through your drawers or anything invasive. But do let him know what is going on with the house and how you are handling it. Also, feel free to ask for his help, opinions, and advice. It will keep you on his good side."

"Okay, I can do that."

"I've got a contract that I copied off the Internet. I've made a few tweaks to include the care of the house as we discussed and the fact that my son will be coming by." She slipped me the four sheets of paper. "Read it over carefully."

I took the papers and was again surprised by the low deposit of five hundred dollars. Glancing up, I took note that she smiled at me.

"When can you move in?" she asked.

It was all happening so fast, but then again, I wasn't buying the house and it was gorgeous and the rent was cheap and even better . . . there were no bars across the street for Bobby to frequent. "I have to give my current landlord thirty days' notice."

"Good," she said. "I'm almost packed."

"Really?" I looked around at the well-stocked kitchen and she laughed.

"Did I not mention that it comes fully furnished? Now, I realize that a woman your age likes to decorate her home her way." She patted my hand. "So you have my blessing to paint and to putter. Any furnishings you don't want, simply call my son and he will pick them up and put them in storage for me."

"What's the downside?" I had to ask.

"You'll have to mow the grass and shovel your own walk," she said. "Or pay someone to do that for you. Mrs. Hamburg two doors down has a sixteen-year-old son who is always looking for money. You can call down there and I'm certain he'd be glad to take over those chores for you. Oh, and did I mention that the garage holds two cars, or in your case one giant Oldsmobile?"

I pulled my checkbook out of my purse. Thankfully I'd put it in there to pay Toby back. Ever since I'd gotten a debit card, I never wrote checks, but now that I'm a small business owner it didn't hurt to have the thing handy at all times.

I signed the contract, wrote out the check, handed both to Mrs. Murphy, and shook her hand. "You made my entire day."

"Oh no, dear, you made mine. I hope you enjoy living here as much as I did."

"I have a feeling I'm going to do just that."

Chapter 18

♂

The next morning found me at a small airport south of Chicago that offered flight lessons and parachute jumps. I was there two hours ahead of time to ensure there was offsite parking and a party bus to take the family to the landing spot. I spoke with the pilot briefly about the flight plan and the timing of the jump. He assured me that Alexander and his girlfriend would arrive about forty-five minutes early to suit up and go over the weather conditions and wind patterns to ensure a safe jump.

"Explain to me what we're doing again," Toby said as he walked into the hangar. Today he wore a wrinkled white polo shirt and a pair of dark blue Dockers with deck shoes. At least he had shaved his usually grizzled chin hair.

"Hi, Toby," I said. "I've finished going over the flight

plan with Jeremy, the pilot." I pointed out the blond in the pressed uniform of the flight school. "He says we're good to go."

"I see, and then what?"

"Then you follow me around as I walk through the party plan."

"And this is of interest to me because?"

"Because I want you to see how excited the family is and how much the potential groom knows about his bride." I glanced over my shoulder to see Alexander coming my way. "Speaking of the potential groom, here he comes now." I stepped away from Toby. "Hi, Alexander. How are you today? Are you ready for the big jump?"

Alex's dark brown eyes sparkled and his face lit up. "I have been so excited I haven't slept a wink in two days."

"Why would you not sleep? Sleep is essential to proper human function," Toby said.

I sent him a look to keep quiet. "Alex, this is Toby Mallard. He is shadowing me today. I hope you don't mind."

"No, of course not," Alex said, and shook Toby's hand. "Alexander Bath, nice to meet you." Then he turned his attention on me. "Here's the ring. Please ensure that Tom gets it. He's Dominica's oldest brother, and if she says yes—"

"When she says yes," I interrupted.

"When she says yes," he repeated, and took a deep breath then let it out slow. "Then Tom will be my best man."

I took the Tiffany blue ring box from him. "May I see it?"

"Please, I'd love to have a woman's reaction."

I opened the box to see a brilliant one-carat stone set

in platinum. "Oh, my." I held it up to the light. "It sparkles so beautifully."

"It's a new cut," Alex said proudly. "See how it domes instead of the standard flat cut? It has ninety facets instead of the standard fifty-two. It's the latest thing. I saw pictures of it on her Pinterest board. Do you think she'll like it?"

"She'll love it," I reassured him with a pat on his back. Then I carefully zipped the ring box into my leather work tote, which carried all of my plans and details for the event. "When is she going to be here?"

He glanced at his watch. "I expect her in the next ten or fifteen minutes."

"Good, I've already briefed your pilot, Jeremy. He tells me all is a go for a perfect jump. He has added head cams to your gear. If she asks why, tell her they are complimentary. Tell her that Jeremy has asked you both to try them out so that he can see how they work. If your videos turn out well, they will be on display to let others know that they can record their jump. Okay?"

"So, wait, he will play our proposal video?"

"No." I shook my head and gave him a reassuring smile. "The video is part of your proposal package. That's only a good excuse for wearing the cameras. Okay?"

"Yes, got it. Sorry, I'm a bit nervous."

"It will be great. You'll see," I said, and gave him a hug. "My videographer, Cesar, is here and he will take footage of the flight up. His assistant, Tomas, will have cameras rolling on the ground to get the families' excitement and point of view." I nodded. "Toby and I are going now. We're going to gather your families at the meet-up point and ensure they get to the drop zone with their signs in hand. I'm on Bluetooth." I tapped on the earpiece of my headset. "If you need me for any reason, you have my cell phone. Dial it. You are my number one priority today. Okay?"

"Okay, thanks."

"Come on, Toby," I said, and put my arm through his. "Let's go get the families."

He took one look at Old Blue and said, "My car is here." He pointed to a dark blue convertible Corvette with tan leather seats. "Shall I follow you?"

"Certainly," I said, and let him go. He did have a gorgeous car and I half wished I was the one driving it. But then I stuck my key in Old Blue's lock and climbed inside to the familiar smell of old vinyl and classic car.

The family meet-up place was the high school parking lot of a nearby town. I had asked a local family restaurant to cater the engagement party after the proposal. The weather cooperated perfectly and a quick check-in with the restaurant reassured me that two large tents were being set up in the field near the drop-off point.

I checked twice that Toby was still following me. It was pretty clear that he still didn't understand the emotions that came with a proposal of marriage. For an obviously brilliant business man, he was clueless when it came to love.

Upon arrival at the parking lot, I was happy to see the party bus already there. Henrique, the driver, stood outside the bus with a sign that said, "Dominica and Alexander's proposal." There were a number of cars already in the lot. I parked Old Blue and waited for Toby to get out and follow me.

"Hi, Henrique, how is it going so far?" I asked.

"Great, the families seem to be getting along fine. I do agree that the champagne at the front of the bus was a good idea."

"Ensure they only get one glass for now. You never know what can happen. If Dominica says no, the ride back might be too emotional. Especially with alcohol in people's systems."

Henrique gave me a one-corner-lifted smile. "My sister Jennifer is inside. She's acting bus director today. She'll ensure that no one steps out of line."

"Perfect."

"And as they enter the bus, they're instructed to take only one glass of champagne for anyone over twenty-one years of age. There are plenty of bottles of water and sodas in the center and the back of the bus."

"Great. Now you know where to meet us?"

"Yes, I have the instructions."

"Good. I'll go in and make sure everyone is getting along. Then I need to get out to the site to check on the tent and other last-minute details."

Two more cars arrived filled with people. I stepped inside the luxury bus. The air-conditioning was running, keeping everyone cool in the fall afternoon warm-up. The inside seats were large and soft. People were laughing and joking around.

"Hello," a lovely young woman with olive skin and black curly hair said. "Welcome aboard. I'm Jennifer and I'm here to ensure you have a great time."

"Hi, Jennifer," I said, and stuck out my hand. "I'm Pepper Pomeroy and I'm the event planner."

"Oh, Miss Pomeroy, of course, welcome. And thank you for hiring Holiday Bus. We spoke on the phone several times."

"Yes, of course," I said. "This is Toby Mallard. He is shadowing me today."

"Hello, Toby, welcome," she said. "Would you like some champagne?"

"No, thanks," he said, his gaze taking in the laughing and joking people. "Is this only one family? They all seem to know each other."

"No, this is both families," Jennifer said. "Plus a group of friends. The families seem to have much in common, right down to their senses of humor. So many came in excited for their role in the proposal."

"Great," I said. "Do you happen to know if Dominica's older brother Tom is on the bus yet?"

"Yes, he was the first. He is in the middle row, right-hand side next to his girlfriend, Marijo." Jennifer pointed him out.

"Thanks, I need to speak to him." As I made my way to Tom, more people arrived on the bus and I was able to observe Jennifer in action. She was very good at her hostess job. Toby squeezed into the driver's area and took it all in. His expression was thoughtful.

I found Tom right where Jennifer said he would be. "Tom?"

"Yes." He looked at me quizzically.

"Hi, I'm Pepper Pomeroy, the event planner Alexander hired."

"Hi," he said, and shook my hand. "This is my girlfriend, Marijo Walters." He pointed to the lovely blonde beside him.

"Hello," I said, and shook her hand as well. "I'm Pepper."

"You have done an amazing job with this so far," Marijo gushed. "I'm totally going to pin your website to my Pinterest board."

"Thanks," I said, and winked at Tom. Hopefully the guy was getting Marijo's not-too-subtle hint that she expected something just as special when he popped the question.

"Listen, I just came from the airport and all is set there."

"Great. How does Alex look? Is he green around the gills or is he excited?"

"He is very excited and if a guy can glow, he's glowing."

"Good. When my sister says yes, he should feel like the luckiest man on earth."

I dug the ring box out of my tote. "He wanted me to give you this."

"Oh, you shouldn't have," Tom teased as he opened the box.

Marijo gasped when she saw the ring. "Oh, my, it's perfect."

"All right, everyone," I said to the bus group in general. "You are all my witnesses. I've given the ring to Tom here. If you don't know, he is Dominica's brother. Say hi, Tom."

"Hi, all," he said.

"When Alex and Dominica hit the ground, Tom is going to give the ring box to Alex, at which point, Alex will drop down on one knee and get his answer." The group on the bus clapped and cheered. "Remember, you all will be holding up the signs asking the important question. I will give you your letter cards and brief you on what to do when you arrive at the drop zone. In the meantime, enjoy yourself. Jennifer and Henrique are here to ensure your comfort. See you soon."

I made my way to the front of the bus and waved for Toby to leave first. We stepped out into the parking lot, then five more guests made their way to the bus.

"Why don't you ride the rest of the way with me," I suggested. "The landing zone is in the country on a gravel road. I wouldn't want to see you chip the paint on your new car."

"Fine," Toby said.

I unlocked his side of the Oldsmobile and then went around the back of the car, unlocked mine, and got in. "What was your impression of the families?" I asked as I pulled out of the parking lot.

"They seemed excited and happy."

"I think I heard a silent, but . . ."

"But," he continued. "It was hard to tell if it was due to the champagne and party bus or the idea of the proposal."

"I see your point," I said, and took the two-lane highway out of town toward the landing zone. "When we get to the landing zone, I'll be handing out posters with letters on them spelling out the words 'Will You Marry Me?' Just observe the entire event. After the proposal, and if Dominica says yes, there will be a tented engagement party. That will be a good time for you to speak to the family and friends one-on-one and get their take on the courtship and romance of the couple. There will be speeches from the parents and the best man, Tom. Listen to them. Watch the couple to get a feel for why courtship and love are important."

"It all seems rather foolish," he said with a frown. "My parents taught me that marriage is a contract between two people. They promise to take care of each other and to support and raise any offspring from the union. If you go into marriage with that logic, it tends to last. That's what they said and I agree. That's why many parts of the world have arranged marriages that work out just fine."

I frowned. "Yes, I suppose that is technically true, but there can be so much more to it than that. If there wasn't, I would be out of a job."

Chapter 19

We arrived in the landing zone and parked in the farmer's field well to the left of the exact landing spot. That way if the wind took them in a wrong direction, they wouldn't get hurt by hitting a car.

The first thing I did was make my way to the party tents. The two large tents connected to create a single room the size of a ballroom. At one end were several overstuffed couches and ottomans arranged on a twenty-by-twenty-foot rug forming a lounge area. Twinkle lights in blue and white draped from the ceiling and a large crystal chandelier hung from the center of the tent. Next were ten round tables that seated ten people each. The tables were covered in three linens. The bottom was dark blue, followed by pale blue, followed by white. The dark blue linens were cut round to match the table. The other two were cut square so that they had corners which crossed in a diamond shape.

The florist placed large but low arrangements of blue statice, white roses, and draped branches that contained blue and white twinkle lights along with crystals to give the centerpiece sparkle and shine.

The caterer was placing silver chargers, pale blue plates, and tiny white presents in stacks in front of each place setting. The presents contained a memento that consisted of a tiny replica of the poster each guest held up while the couple parachuted down.

On the final end of the tent was a small ten-by-ten-foot dance floor. The DJ was set up off to the side and a large screen filled the back of the dance area with a slide show of the couple at various points in their lives together.

I spoke to the caterer and the disc jockey to ensure all was going well. Then I glanced at my watch and saw that it was time for the bus to arrive. I went out to Old Blue and pulled out a megaphone and the large posters with the letters on them. Toby leaned against the car with his hands in his pockets.

"The bus is here."

"Thanks," I said. "Can you get the stepladder and follow me?"

"Sure, why not." Toby pulled the four-foot ladder from the back of Old Blue's trunk. The center of the field had a large bull's-eye on it to give the jumpers a target to aim for when they landed. I waved for the family to follow me and we made a mini parade of about seventy-five people. I placed them in rows and handed them the cards.

Then I took the ladder from Toby, moved it toward the target and set it up. "Okay everyone, if I can have your attention, please," I said into the megaphone once I got to the top of the ladder. "Let's have a practice run. Back row hold up your cards over your heads."

The cards read "Dominica Barret."

"Perfect," I said into the phone. "Now, second row, please hold up your cards over your head." The cards went up and said, "Will ouY." Okay, that wasn't good. I put down the megaphone and called Toby over. "Fix the three on the right. It should be *Y-o-u* not *o-u-Y*."

"Got it," he said, and went over and had them switch cards.

I picked up the megaphone. "One more time, second row, please raise your cards up over your heads." This time the words were correct. "Good. Now, last row, please raise your cards."

The cards correctly spelled, "Marry me?" I was proud. Everyone was grinning. I climbed down and checked the time. The plane should have taken off and would arrive at jumping altitude in five minutes. "All right, everyone. Stay in your places."

Toby followed me back to Old Blue. "They are all so excited. I've heard them saying that Alexander and Dominica have been dating for five years."

"Yes," I said, and opened the trunk of my car. "Can you help me with this?" We each took the handle of a big old green and white cooler.

"What do you have in here?" Toby asked as we both strained to lift it out of the car.

"Drinks," I said. "I need to take this to the family." We crossed the drive and the field by waddling along and occasionally putting down the cooler for a moment and then picking it back up. The day's heat had begun to set in. The wind was still relatively calm and the air smelled of fall grasses. I could hear cicadas and crickets under the low hush of the families talking and laughing.

We put the cooler down and my cell phone beeped. "The plane should reach jump altitude in a few minutes," I announced. "In the meantime, have some water. We don't need anyone passing out and dropping their card."

The crowd clapped and cheered. I leaned over to Toby. "Could you help me hand these out?" Inside the cooler were ice and nearly a hundred mini bottles of water. It took us five minutes to get everyone their drinks.

"All right, everyone," I said into the megaphone. "Listen up. I just got a text telling me they have reached the jump height. Water bottles down and get ready."

I studied the sky and spotted the plane in the distance. My phone chirped. "And they've jumped!" I climbed up on the ladder. "Okay, row one—go!" They all flipped their cards and were still in order. I counted ten seconds. "Row two—go!" They all cheered and raised their cards. I counted another ten seconds. "Last row—go!"

Everyone cheered and pumped their cards. The message was dead on. I texted the pilot. "Are you good?"

"Roger that," he texted back.

"The pilot sees us and can clearly read the sign," I said into the megaphone. The cheering grew louder as the parachutes were pulled and the couple floated down. "Hold your place," I warned them. With all the excitement I didn't want anyone to rush up and ruin the message. "Hold!"

Alexander had a red and yellow parachute. Dominica had a pink and blue chute. I grabbed my binoculars and waved my hand over my head. Alex sent me a thumbs-up. "Yes!" I grabbed the megaphone. "I got a thumbs-up from Alex!"

The families started dancing in place, waving their posters over their heads. "Now, turn your cards over!" I shouted. They turned them over and the words *Congratulations, Alex and Dominica* came into view.

I grabbed the binoculars and zoomed into Dominica's face. "She's crying," I said. "I hope to goodness those are tears of joy."

Alex landed first. Moments later Dominica landed. Tom dropped his poster and rushed out to help Alex untangle from his chute. Another guy ran out and untangled Dominica. Tomas zoomed in with his video camera. I got off the ladder and went to Dominica.

"Stay right here," I said, and stopped her. Then I motioned for her girlfriend Heather to stand by her. I could see that Dominica was shaking. "Are you okay?"

"Yes," she said. "Definitely!"

The families surrounded her as Tom gave the box to Alex. He strode toward her, got down on one knee, and opened the ring box. "Dominica Barret, will you do me the honor of marrying me?"

Her trembling hands went to her mouth. Tears welled up in her eyes. The crowd grew silent. "Yes, Alex, oh yes!" She threw her arms around him and he stood, picking her up and twirling her. There was not a dry eye in the crowd as he stopped and let her down slowly, and then placed the ring on her left ring finger.

"You have made me the luckiest man in the world."

The families clapped happily, smiles all around. I went back to the ladder and climbed up two steps to be seen above the crowd. "Congratulations to Alex and Dominica!" I said into the megaphone. The crowd cheered again. "Now, please follow Alex and Dominica over to the white tents for dinner, dancing, and the engagement party."

I watched as the entire group followed the happy couple across the field, over the gravel drive to the tents beyond. Cesar appeared near the cars and gave me a thumbs-up. I smiled and returned the gesture. Cesar was my videographer of choice and he had been late to the field because he had been at the airport pretending to be a "Documentary Videographer" working on a short film for the jump school. He was really there to film Alex and Dominica preparing for the Big Leap. Cesar is a good sport about most of the events that I plan, but was adamant that he was not about to jump out of a plane to get the shot of the moment that Dominica saw the cards.

That was okay with me. I was certain the helmet cams would catch the shot. From the look on Alex's face, it didn't matter if they did or didn't. The whole thing had me grinning.

"That was quite a success," Toby said as he stood beside the stepladder. "I certainly got a better understanding of the emotion behind what it is that you do."

"Good," I said, and folded up the ladder to take back to Old Blue. "Why don't you go on in to the tent, get a drink, and see if you can find out a little more about the courtship. Marriage may be a contract as you described, but it is not cold or bloodless. The courtship aspect builds trust and affection. It allows people to see if they have things in common."

"Perhaps, but, as I mentioned, in many countries people have arranged marriages. These are often statistically more successful than marriages based on emotion."

"Toby." I blew out a breath. "Unless you want a mail-order bride who doesn't speak English very well, you need to truly understand how courtship and love work into marriage. Now go." I shooed him off. "Enjoy yourself. Meet people. Get their take on the issue."

"Are you leaving?" he asked, his expression confused.

"No, I'll be over there in a bit. First I need to pack up and such."

"Okay." He shrugged, shoved his hands in his pockets, and wandered after the crowd.

I put the ladder in the trunk of my car, gathered up all the posters, and stacked them in the back as well. Finally, I emptied the cooler of the ice and packed it away.

The jump school had taken care of the parachute gear and the bull's-eye tarp. I stopped, stretched, and lifted my face to the sun. Another successful event. I pulled out my phone and called Gage.

"Hey, beautiful," he answered.

"Hi," I said as a warm feeling washed over me.

"How did your event go?"

"Great," I said, and leaned against the car. "Dominica was crying, Alex was crying. In fact I don't think there was a dry eye in the field."

"Isn't the saying 'there wasn't a dry eye in the house'?"

"Yes, well, this was entirely outside, so . . ." I let the words trail off.

"I get it. I was teasing," he said. "I'm glad it went so well. Want to go out tonight and celebrate? I know this nice little Greek restaurant that you might like. I know you love hummus."

"How did you know?"

"I pay attention," he said.

"Bobby never took me to anyplace that might resemble a restaurant that wasn't a franchise."

"I know," Gage said softly. "Let's not talk about him. Okay?"

"Sure, I'm sorry." I bit my bottom lip. "I would love to go out and celebrate with you tonight. I have more great news, other than how well the Big Leap went, but it can wait until I see you."

"Well, then I'm looking forward to your news and seeing you in something sexy."

I couldn't help the smile that crossed my face. "Is that a hint that I should dress up a bit?"

"It's a date, Pepper."

"Then I'm looking forward to seeing you in something sexy as well."

"It's a deal. I'll pick you up at eight."

Chapter 20

The doorbell rang. I opened it to find Gage leaning against the doorjamb wearing a black velvet suit coat, a light blue pinstriped shirt, and a pair of black dress pants. His hair was perfectly groomed with a side part, which caused his bangs to flirtatiously cover his forehead.

"Wow," we said at the same time.

I smiled and did a flirty turn so that my black fit-and-flare dress's skirt swished around my knees. The neckline was U-shaped, giving a hint of cleavage and showing off the red glass beaded necklace I wore. A pair of pointed-toe black pumps with kitten heels finished off the simple ensemble.

"Very nice," Gage said, and pulled his arms out from

behind his back. In one hand he had a gorgeous bouquet of flowers and in the other a nice bottle of Cabernet.

"Oh, for me?" I sounded as surprised as I felt.

"Yes, for you, silly," he said, and stepped inside, wrapped both arms around me and gave me a kiss, which I felt clear to my toes. "That's for you, too. Anytime you need or want it."

My brain fell out of my head and I stood there smiling.

"Are you going to take them?" he asked and waved the flowers under my nose.

"Right, sure." I took the flowers. "Let me put these in water." He followed me into the kitchen and tucked the wine inside my refrigerator as I grabbed a glass cup from the cupboard, filled it halfway with water, and put the flowers inside. "Tada!" I said, and waved my hands like a magician's assistant. "Done and done."

He backed me up against the counter, put both hands on the countertop beside me, and leaned in. "You are something, Pepper Pomeroy."

I wrapped my arms around his neck. "Thank you." I planted a hot kiss on him. "So are you, Gage."

He shivered after my kiss and I found it entirely too endearing. "Come on." He took my hand. "Let's get out of here and celebrate, because if we don't go soon, we're never going to leave."

"Oh, no, and then my sexy dress would go to waste." I batted my eyelashes.

"Trust me, even if I took it off you right now, it didn't go to waste." He tugged me through the doorway. "I think

I will have that cute little twirl seared into my memory forever."

"In a good way, I hope," I said as I locked my apartment door.

"Are you fishing for compliments?"

"What?" I froze. "No, no, I wasn't."

He winked and kissed my forehead. "Then let me set you straight right now. You are the most beautiful woman I've ever laid eyes on, Pepper."

"Thank you." I bit my lower lip to keep myself from denying his words.

He smiled and I knew he caught me trying not to counter him. "Come on, dinner awaits."

* * *

The restaurant was small, as promised. All the tables were filled with couples and groups. Everyone was well dressed and gorgeous in the flickering candlelight. Even though the tables were full, the conversations were low and intimate. Not a single child or French fry in sight.

"Marcos," Gage said and hugged the maître' d. "How are you? You look great, my friend. Let me introduce you to my date. This is Pepper Pomeroy. Pepper this is Marcos Steponoplios."

"How do you do?" I asked, and went to shake his hand. Instead of shaking my hand he kissed it and I felt the heat of a blush rush up to the roots of my hair.

"Gage has told me all about you." He winked. "It appears every word is true. Come, let me seat you someplace nice."

Marcos was young and handsome with thick black hair that curled at the nape. His eyes were dark brown and dancing with an inner joy. He had wide shoulders and a narrow frame and could have passed for a movie star. So, of course, I followed him. Gage put his hand on the small of my back and reminded me who I was with—not that I forgot or anything.

"Here is the best seat in the house." Marcos put us in the corner farthest from the kitchen. The table was small and cozy, with windows on both walls so that you could see the lights of the sidewalk. It was dark and the city street held a quiet mystery. There were curtains as well if you wished to close the table off from the rest of the world. "My lady," Marcos said, and held out my chair. I sat and he tucked me in properly, and then placed a black napkin on my lap. "George is your waiter tonight. If he gives you any problems, let me know."

Marcos handed us red cloth-covered menus, winked at Gage, and left.

"He's a nice guy," I said, and leaned forward. "How do you know him, again?"

Gage smiled. "I bring all my dates here."

"Oh," I said, and sat back a little disappointed. Gage took my hand in his.

"Just kidding." He stroked his thumb along my knuckles and I felt a shiver of desire. "We went to school together."

"Okay, better," I said. Then I paused and leaned forward, concerned. "I know you've had several girlfriends. All I've ever had was Bobby. I'm not good at casual. Wait!"

I held up the hand he had been holding. "I can't say I'm not good at casual, not really. All I can say is that I'm not used to it. There are things I might not get."

"Such as my joking about all my girlfriends," Gage said, then leaned his elbow on the table and rested his chin on his hand. "I've only had four, Pepper, and none of them lasted longer than three months."

"Wait, I thought you were serious about Angela Davis."

"That was our junior year in high school and I liked her because she reminded me of you." He sat back and picked up his menu. "She didn't like the fact that she reminded me of you and dumped me."

"Huh," I said, as our waiter showed up carrying a tray with two glasses of ice-cold water, two wineglasses, and a bottle of red wine.

"Good evening, I'm George and I'll be your server tonight. I've brought you water and Marcos has sent you this Cabernet." He silently went to work, placing the glasses on the table, then he showed the wine label to Gage, popped open the cork, and showed that to him as well, then finally poured a tiny bit in both wineglasses. I followed Gage's actions and swirled the wine, sniffed it, then tasted it. It smelled of oak and berries and left a soft buttery taste on the tongue.

"Very good," Gage said.

George nodded and poured more wine in our glasses. Then he left.

"I keep forgetting you know about wine," I said.

"I know about a lot of things, which you will learn along

the way," Gage said, and winked. "Now what sounds good to you?"

For the first time I noticed there was no pricing on my menu. That left me feeling odd. I wanted to be polite and ask for neither the cheapest nor the most expensive items. I put down the menu. "Surprise me."

"Ha!" Gage teased, his gaze sparkling in the lamp light. "You don't like the fact that there are no prices on your menu."

I blushed again and tried to hide it by sipping my wine. "Maybe, or maybe I'm testing you. Maybe I want to see how much you know about me and about the menu here."

Gage shook his head and waved George over. Then he ordered for us both, starting with the promised hummus and pita bread.

"To celebrating your latest Perfect Proposal." He lifted his wineglass.

"To Alex and Dominica, long may their marriage last and bring them both joy." We touched glasses and took a drink. "I have more news," I said.

Gage reached over and took my hand in his. "Okay, tell me."

"I've found a new place to rent."

"That's great!" He squeezed my hand and I felt truly connected to someone for the first time in years. "Where?"

"It's in Park Ridge. Remember I told you I might be rooming with an older woman? Well, you won't believe this, but Detective Murphy's mom is the owner of the house and she is moving to Florida for good. She's willing to rent her home to me. Fully furnished if I need it, but she's willing to let me redecorate to my heart's content."

"That's fantastic," Gage said.

"And the best part is that there is no bar within a half mile of the house."

Gage lifted his glass. "Here's to being Bobby free."

"Amen," I said, and we touched glasses again and I sipped. "Also it seems that Detective Murphy has a suspect arrested in the bridal shop murder."

"Who?"

"Remember I told you about Vidalia's assistant, Theresa, and her odd boyfriend? Well, apparently this guy Thad stole the pieces from the shop while Vidalia was out getting coffee. Detective Murphy thinks that Eva caught him and pulled the knife, hoping to intimidate Thad into giving back the stolen goods."

"That's a little crazy, don't you think? I mean, why didn't she just call the cops? We all have cell phones. She could have videotaped him stealing them and then called the police."

I frowned. "That does make more sense than grabbing a knife and trying to threaten him." I rested my chin in my hand. "Why would you grab a knife?"

"What did Detective Murphy say?"

"He said he thinks they fought and Thad accidentally killed Eva in the struggle, and then ran away."

"I suppose that could happen." Gage shrugged. "Seems a little out there."

I couldn't agree more. George brought our first course

and our conversation turned to Gage and the work he was doing at the warehouse. The best part about his being in the prop business was that he knew about all the movies being shot in town, and all the new plays and musicals. He had the best behind-the-scenes stories.

"Not to talk business on this lovely date," I said when the conversation lulled. "But Sunday is Mary's proposal. We have the theatre booked. Do you have the props picked out?"

"Yes," Gage said. "I've got those great 1920s prop palms to put near the stage. Plus, everyone entering the theatre will put on costumes like you requested."

"Now their friends and family will know to come early so they can get ready. I've got a few actors set to pretend to come in when Mary and Joe do, so it appears as if strangers are going through the same thing, but the theatre will actually be closed to the public."

"So most of the theatre will be full already," Gage deduced.

"Yes, there will be champagne flutes at the entrance to the theatre and the lights will be low with someone set to take everyone to their seats."

"So he doesn't notice his family and friends," Gage said.

"Exactly. They will all be instructed to face forward in the hope that he will not notice anyone but Mary and perhaps the actors who will be seated around him."

"What else do you need from me, prop wise?" Gage asked.

"You've got that lovely 1920s microphone and stand, and then the chair I picked out the other day. The moment Mary and Joe are seated, the spotlight will go to the front stage and the emcee will come in to introduce the film and do a short interview with a Humphrey Bogart impersonator."

"*Casablanca* is the perfect film, romantic for the women and yet war torn for the guys." Gage waggled his right eyebrow. "Nice."

"Thanks." I blushed. "When the movie hits intermission, the lights will come back up on the stage and the emcee will come out. He will make an announcement saying that a prize awaits the people in Mary and Joe's seats. A spotlight will go on Mary and Joe and they will be instructed to come up on stage where Mary will propose."

"Brilliant," Gage said. "I'll have everything packed up and over there two hours before the event."

"Thanks."

He took a sip of his wine, and then looked me in the eye. "Now, about your new place. When are you moving?"

"I gave my landlord thirty days' notice, but I can move anytime."

"Good," he said. "That's great. I've got a truck and some guys who can help move your stuff."

"That would be awesome," I agreed. "How does the end of the month look to you?"

"It looks great," he said and lifted his wineglass. "Here's to fresh starts."

"To fresh starts," I agreed, touched his glass, and took a sip. Things were moving fast, but in a very good direction.

Chapter 21

I met Toby at the coffee shop near Bridal Dreams the next afternoon. "So what did you think of the engagement?" I asked as I handed him a large pumpkin spice latte.

"I can see what you mean about how they looked at each other," he said, and blew out a breath. He sat back in his chair and threw his arm over the back of the chair next to him. "I can't help but think they are the exception to the rule. It's just a bad business decision to base a contract as important as marriage on chemical reactions of the body."

I sat down and clutched my coffee. "Wow, that's what you think of love? It's just chemical reactions?"

"Research shows that we are attracted by pheromones created to appeal to the opposite sex with the optimum DNA."

I smiled. "What about youth and beauty?" I asked, playing devil's advocate. "You know. Signs of good health, fertility?"

"Yes, there must be attraction," he said. "For example, you are an attractive woman."

Why did that make me blush? Plus, I knew that my blotchy redhead blush was not particularly attractive.

"But," he continued, "if I were to ask you to marry me right now, you would say . . ."

"What?" I shook my head, shocked by the thought. "No."

"Why not? Your children wouldn't want for money or care. They could go to the finest schools. Not have to rack up college bills. You wouldn't have to work another day in your life."

"I love my job," I bristled. "And I don't know you."

"You are intelligent. I'm sure you did an online search of me when you were doing your research on Laura."

"You don't have a very big online footprint," I pointed out. "Which means you are either very private or uninterested in staying in touch with your friends." I paused. "Or you don't have any friends. I couldn't tell."

"You did a credit report, right?"

"It's part of what I do before I take on a client, yes," I said.

"So you know that I'm wealthy and stable and don't have an arrest record."

"But there are so many other factors to marriage. Ideally you want the marriage to last forever."

"Exactly, that's why it shouldn't be based on attraction or current health. That goes away."

"You need to meet my parents," I said, and pushed back from the table. "Remember the stars that Alexander and Dominica had in their eyes? My parents still have them after thirty-five years of marriage. I have to tell you, Toby, I believe in that."

"I'm still not convinced. You said there was another event you were planning?"

"Yes, please come. We'll meet again after and continue this conversation." I reached into my bag. "I bought these poppers for when he says yes." I put a handful of colorful exploding confetti poppers on the table.

Toby picked one up. "Are those fireworks?"

"No, they are not fireworks, per se. I did the research to find ones that are permissible inside the theater. But they do have a pretty good pop. Want to try one?"

Toby shook his head. "No, thanks. I'll wait."

"Okay." I pulled them off the table and stuck them in the pockets of my jacket. "Listen, I need to go. I want to see a friend. I expect to see you at Mary's thing, okay? I really think you'll get it with more exposure." I patted his hand. "You're a nice guy, Toby. You deserve stars in your eyes."

I gathered up my tote bag and coffee and waved good-bye. I wanted to see Vidalia. Since I had heard that Thad was arrested, I wanted to know how she was. Did she agree with the detective? Was she relived to have Thad in jail or was she still worried about the killer being out there? Besides, I never did like Vidalia's explanation of the third coffee being for her mom. Something was off about the entire thing and I needed to figure out what.

Old Blue was parked on the side of the road just down from the coffee shop. Instead of driving, I decided to walk and gauge the time and distance between the coffee shop and Bridal Dreams. I put more money in the meter and checked the time on my phone. I had to figure Vidalia was slower than me since she would have been carrying a coffee tray and she is shorter than me with a smaller stride.

I leisurely strolled the five blocks to the front of the shop and checked my watch. It was a ten-minute walk. I studied the building for a moment. Maybe it would be a good idea to walk back to the coffee shop and average the time.

It occurred to me that the baristas might know something about that day. Of course, Detective Murphy told me not to bother talking to them. I had to assume he probably already interviewed them, but I couldn't shake the thought of that third cup.

I walked back into the coffee shop. Toby was gone and most of the people who had stopped in were gone as well. I walked up to the counter. "Hi."

"Need another latte?" the barista asked. He was lanky with a full head of floppy blond hair. His blue eyes sparkled with youth and energy.

"No, um, actually, I was wondering if you know Vidalia or Eva Svetkovska."

"Sure, Vidalia comes in here all the time," He said. "Too bad about Eva, She was a nice lady. Makes you think more about safety, though, when something like that happens in your neighborhood."

"I know, right? I just walked to the shop and back and I felt safe. Is this area known for crime?"

"Oh, no," he said, and wiped down the counter with a bar rag. "Never had any crime before Eva's death."

"Were you working that day?"

"Yeah, I work here most afternoons during the week," he said. "We're small. There are a couple of girls on the morning shift, me on the afternoon, and the boss man comes and goes. I remember serving Vidalia that day. She was happy, chatty. I forget what we talked about but I remember she was in a good mood."

"I'm the one who found Eva," I said. "I'm Pepper Pomeroy."

"Hi, Pepper. Sam," he said, and pointed at his name tag. "Finding Eva like that must have been a bad experience. Did you know her?"

"No, my sister is getting married and we had an appointment. When no one was around when we got there, I went looking."

"Oh, you must have been the appointment that Vidalia said she was running late for when she ordered her take-home coffees."

"I think so, no one else was there but us—my sister, my mom, and me. When Vidalia came in, she was carrying three cups of coffee. Do you remember her ordering three? Was that normal?"

"Yeah, I remember," he said, and leaned his elbow on the glass case containing baked goods and yogurt. "Their order is almost always the same—one large coffee, black, and one large coffee with cream. It almost never varies." He paused. "Unless they're expecting company. Once in a while Vidalia orders a large café mocha like she did that day."

"Huh, she said that the extra coffee was for Eva because she likes two sometimes."

He squinted his eyes and scowled. "No, that's not right. Eva likes her coffee black. There's no way she would want a café mocha."

"She must have gotten mixed up," I said thoughtfully. "It must have been quite a shock to find out your mother was murdered in the alley while you were out getting coffee."

"Yeah," he agreed, and shook his head. "Heck of a thing. Would make anyone mix things up, I guess."

"Anyway, thanks for the info." I straightened.

"No problem, you've been in here a few times," he said, and grinned. "I like to find out more about my customers. Keeps things personal and real."

I blushed at his warm gaze. "Right. Coffee's great here. Thanks for the chat."

"See you soon, Pepper."

I left the coffee shop and strolled back toward Bridal Dreams. Vidalia lied about the coffee. Why? She didn't seem like a person who would murder her mother. Was she protecting someone? I didn't think she would try to protect Thad. So why lie about the coffee?

Maybe the murderer wasn't Thad at all. In that case there was a serious injustice being done. I really needed to talk to Vidalia. Maybe if I pushed her, she would at least confirm that she lied about the coffee.

As I headed out of the parking lot, I noticed that an alley ran behind the coffee shop. Was that another way to get to the bridal shop? I followed the alley and saw that I could get to the bridal shop from its alley. I turned on my heel and walked back to the coffee shop via the alley. There were several unmarked buildings in this area, with nothing more than an address and dark windows. You could practically get from the coffee shop to the bridal shop without being seen.

That was a wild thought. I bet anyone who lived or worked in the area knew about taking the back way. In fact, Detective Murphy had said that Thad had admitted to running through the alley after he stole the things from the bridal shop.

Still, I just couldn't see Thad murdering anyone, let alone Eva. He didn't seem strong enough either physically or mentally. I walked the area a few more times and realized it was faster to take the alleys. So why did Vidalia come back the street way? I mean, wouldn't she have cut through the alley if she knew she was running late?

Did she know something? Was Vidalia careful to come in through the front door so she wouldn't see anyone in the alley? It was getting dark and I really needed to go in and see if Vidalia had time to answer some questions. There was no way I was going to wait for my next dress fitting three weeks from now.

I turned on my heel and headed back toward the alley's

opening. After seeing the bolt on the back door, I was pretty certain Vidalia wouldn't open it to a knock when it was getting dark. That meant I had to go in through the front door.

Anton stepped out of the back of one of the dark-doored buildings. "What's going on, Pepper?" he asked. "What are you looking for?"

"I'm sorry." I paused mid-step, embarrassed that he had seen me in the alley.

"You've been walking the alley for the last half hour," he said. "Why?"

Okay, it was downright creepy that he had been watching me and I hadn't even known it. Wait, he could see me through the darkened windows. That meant he might have seen someone besides Thad in the alley the day Eva was killed.

"Is this the back of your furniture shop?" I asked.

"Yes." His gaze darkened.

"So you really are just down from Bridal Dreams," I muttered. "You could have seen whoever was in the alley that day."

"What are you thinking, Pepper?" His look turned eerily deadly.

Reality hit me like ice water down my spine and I couldn't stop the words from spilling out of my mouth. "Oh, my goodness, you killed Eva, didn't you?"

Chapter 22

Anton jumped forward and grabbed me. I kicked and yelled, but he wrapped his big hand around my mouth and I struggled to breathe as he dragged me into the back of the furniture restoration shop. The smell of varnish was so intense it made my eyes water and nearly took my breath away.

I kept struggling, but Anton was strong. He pushed me into a chair and leaned in close to my ear. "You can scream all you want, no one can hear you. The buildings on either side of me are empty."

When he took his hand off my mouth, I screamed anyway and pushed to my feet. He smacked me hard, making my eyes water, and shoved me back into the chair.

"Why did you kill Eva?" I said to distract myself from the pain. "What did she do to you?"

He pulled up a chair across from mine. "I did not hate her, if that is what you imagine. As mother-in-laws go, she was fine."

"Then why?"

"Eva was not firm enough with her son. Vlad is lazy and no good, and yet Eva kept giving him money. Vidalia works hard—very hard. She saw nothing from her mother. Eva kept saying Vidalia didn't need anything." He sat down. "But you see, it is not the need for money. It is recognition of how hard my wife and I work."

"But Eva gave Vidalia sole ownership of the bridal shop, isn't that recognition?" I asked as I noticed my surroundings. There were several work benches with chairs on top in various stages of repair. The strong smell of varnish emanated from a nearby table that appeared to be freshly coated. Tools were scattered about. I noted several that might help me should I make my move.

"That is where she crossed the line." Anton spit on the floor beside him. "Eva had been talking about how she felt guilty for not giving Vladimir one last chance to redeem himself—by letting him share in the workload of the shop." He sneered. "As if the lazy brother would actually do the work. I knew he would ruin it all. All the work my wife has put into the shop. I urged my wife to speak to her mother. Eva kept talking about making the change to her will and said she had to do it, that it was the right thing."

"Vidalia didn't talk to her mother about it, did she? And you couldn't let Eva change her will, could you?" I said. "You couldn't let Vidalia lose half the shop to Vlad's wasteful ways."

"No, I could not let that happen. A man looks out for his wife."

"Why didn't you just talk to her?"

"I had finally convinced Vidalia to speak to her mother. I wanted to be there to ensure my wife did not back down. Eva was a strong personality. Vidalia respected her mother. It was difficult for her to push for what she deserved."

"That's why Vidalia had the third coffee," I said, putting things together. "You were supposed to meet with her that day."

"Yes, after your appointment," he said. "But I couldn't wait. I had a bad feeling that Vidalia would back down, again. I knew Theresa was out that day. When Vidalia went to get coffee, I stopped at the bridal shop to see Eva. I intended to scare her a bit, before Vidalia returned. I wanted to make sure she knew that there would be consequences if she didn't listen to my wife." He paused, dragged in a heavy breath, and stood. "But Eva said she would call the police because I had threatened her." He started to pace. "Worse, she said she would tell Vidalia. I couldn't let her do that. I couldn't lose my wife and all we'd worked for." I could tell from his body language that he was getting worked up and that frightened me. I kept one eye on Anton and another looking for a way out before things went very bad.

"Why did you have to kill her?" I pushed. My body started to shake from fear. I put my hands in my jacket pockets to hide the trembling and realized that I had the poppers in my pocket.

He grabbed a roll of metallic duct tape from the top of one of the work benches and walked toward me, his manner suddenly cold and purposeful. "I grabbed her to shake some sense into her, but she fought back. I had taken the knife to scare her, but she went too far. I couldn't have it. I refused to let her ruin everything."

"So you killed her," I said, and watched his emotionless approach.

"And now I will kill you, to save everything. It is not that I wish you harm, Pepper Pomeroy, but I cannot let you ruin things."

When he leaned toward me and ripped the tape from the roll, I pulled a popper out and broke it, pushing the explosive streamer into his face.

He shouted and put his hand over his eyes. I didn't waste a moment. Anton stood between me and the back door, so I headed toward the front of the shop. The place was a typical workshop with band saws, workbenches, and tools everywhere. There were pieces of furniture in various stages of repair scattered about. My panicked mind grew frustrated at the obstacle course.

I pushed aside a chair, skirted around a table, and headed toward the front door. Anton recovered quickly. I could feel him right behind me. My heart pounded. My eyes were focused on my escape.

Do not look back. If you look back, you waste time. It was the biggest mistake movie heroines made. I shoved chairs and end tables behind me, hoping they would slow him down.

"Stop!" Anton shouted.

It felt like forever, but I battled my way to the front door. I could feel his breath on the back of my neck. I grabbed the handle, but the door was locked with a bolt. My hands shook as I struggled to unbolt the door.

"You won't get away," I heard him say. His voice was so close.

There was a cast iron coatrack near the door. I grabbed it and shoved it at him. Then I threw open the bolt and ran out screaming. "Fire!"

My brain remembered the weirdest things and I kept shouting. "Help! Fire!" I had read somewhere once that people respond to shouts of *Fire!* better than to someone yelling *Help me!*

There was a couple at the end of the block who turned at the sound of my shouting. "Call the police," I begged. "Call the fire department."

I looked behind me. Anton was steps away. I sprinted toward the couple.

"There is no fire," he shouted to the couple. "She is crazy. Do not listen to her."

I got behind the young man and held on to him. "Please help."

Thankfully the young guy, who was a nice sturdy size, blocked Anton from grabbing me.

"Dude, whatever is going on here, stop. I'm not going to let you get to this girl," the young man said.

"I've got 911 on the line," the girl he was with chimed in. She stepped behind both me and the man she was with and put the phone to her ear. "Yes, we are at 345 Brocton. We need police now!" Her eyes went straight to Anton. "Yes, I feel as if I'm in danger."

Anton stopped short. "This is none of your business," he said to the couple, his gaze shifting from one to the other. I could see him trying to figure out how to get to me.

My instinct was to run, but I knew if I left the couple, Anton might be able to outrun me. If I stayed here, it meant he was really close, but I had witnesses.

"I'm making it my business," the young man said, and crossed his arms over his chest and stood with his feet spread wide. "Clearly, she does not want you to touch her."

"What's going on?" A second man came out of the shop we were in front of. "Is everything okay?"

"It's fine," Anton said.

"There's a fire," the woman said. I smiled at her. Her blue eyes sparkled with intelligence as she continued to stay on the line with the 911 operator. "I've called 911."

"There is no fire," Anton said, his gaze wild. "This is none of your business. Pepper, come with me."

"No!" I said, and grabbed the back of the young man's shirt and hung on. "He killed Eva." I pointed at Anton.

Sirens could be heard in the distance. Anton panicked and ran off. The young man started after him so I let go. The shopkeeper ran after the man and Anton. The young woman and I watched as they disappeared into the nearest alley.

Shaking, my knees gave way and I sat down hard. Two police cars screamed to a halt beside us. The fire marshal was not far behind. The first two policemen got out of their cars and raced off in the direction of the men. The young woman squatted next to me.

"Are you okay?" she asked. "Are you hurt?"

"No, no, I'm not hurt." I shook my head. "He scared me."

"My name is Amanda," she said. "I'll stay with you. Is there anyone I can call?"

I managed to get my phone out of my pocket, but my hands shook too hard to dial. "Here," I handed her my phone. "Please call my parents. They are listed under my emergency numbers."

She quickly flipped through my phone to the emergency contact numbers and dialed my mom. Amanda put the phone on speaker and handed it to me as soon as it started to ring.

"Thanks," I said.

The second set of policemen approached, followed by the fire marshal. "What happened?" the first cop asked.

"Hello?" my mom answered her phone.

"Hi, Mom," I said as the young girl stood and stepped to the side to explain why she had called 911. "I need you and Dad to come down to Bridal Dreams."

"What's the matter?" Mom asked, and her tone was troubled so I knew I did not sound good.

"Thad didn't kill Eva. Anton did."

"Who is Anton and how do you know this?" Mom asked.

"Anton is Vidalia's husband," I said wearily.

"Oh, Pepper, what have you gotten yourself into?"

"I have to go, Mom, the police are here. Please come down. I'm in no shape to drive home." I hung up.

The fire marshal hunkered down beside me. "Are you hurt?" he asked. His eyes were a soft light brown and his skin golden olive. Black curly hair peeked out from under his uniform hat.

"I don't think so," I said. "Mostly scared." I tried to get up.

"Stay where you are until the paramedics can check you out." He put his hand gently on my shoulder.

"Okay, miss," The policeman came over after he finished speaking with Amanda. "You were yelling fire, is that right?"

"Yes, I heard it is better to yell *fire* than *help*. People respond faster. All I could think to do was yell fire."

"Okay, that's fine," he said. "Is there a fire?"

"No," I said, and apologized to the fire marshal. "There is no fire. Anton kidnapped me and I got away and wanted someone to help me."

"Okay," The fire marshal nodded and patted my shoulder. "I'm going to leave you in the hands of Officer Grumpki. The EMTs are pulling up now. Do not move until they can check you out. Okay?"

"Okay." I took a deep breath and hugged my knees to my chest. I looked at the officer. "Anton killed Eva."

"Let's start from the beginning," he said, his gaze flat and serious. "Tell me what happened. What is your name?"

"Pepper Pomeroy."

"All right, Miss Pomeroy, what happened here today?"

I explained what happened from the time I left the coffee shop until I escaped from Anton. When I got that far, I saw that the first two policemen had emerged from the alley with a cuffed and dirty Anton. The young man and the shopkeeper followed, looking fierce.

My parents' car shrieked up onto the curb. "Pepper," Mom said as she and Dad rushed to my side. "Oh, thank goodness you are okay." She threw her arms around me and I started crying.

The EMTs approached and cautioned me to remain seated. They did a quick check of my pulse and my breathing and asked if I was in any pain. All the while my mom held my hand. Dad had gone over to where the policemen were interviewing the shopkeeper and Amanda's young man.

"Looks like a simple case of adrenaline overload," the EMT pronounced and handed me an ice pack. "Put this on your cheek. You're going to have a bit of a shiner for a few days." He stood and addressed my mom. "Her pupils look okay so I doubt she has a concussion. It might still be good to keep an eye on her. If she has any further symptoms, take her to the ER right away."

"Okay," Mom said and squeezed my hand.

"Anton hit me," I said, and placed the ice pack on the side of my face.

The paramedic continued to talk to Mom. "Take her home and see that she gets rest." Then he turned to me; his blue eyes and blond hair looked good against his dark blue uniform. "When you have that kind of scare, injuries can remain hidden for a while. If later tonight you have any problems like sharp pains or headaches, I want you to go to the emergency room immediately. Do you understand?"

"Yes, thank you," I said, and he helped me to my feet. It took a moment to get my balance, but then I was okay.

Mom wrapped her arms around me. "Oh, sweetie, I'm glad you are all right. Let's take you home."

"Thanks, Mom," I said, and let her lead me toward the cops and my father. The car with Anton left and a strange sadness engulfed me.

Dad looked grim as he approached us. "They said we could take you home. I have Officer Grumpki's card. He'll be calling in the morning to ask you more questions."

"I imagine your Detective Murphy will be calling as well," Mom said as she walked me toward their car, her arm around me.

"Poor Vidalia," I said. "I don't think she has a clue that Anton killed her mother." I let them tuck me into the backseat of their Buick. "Can you imagine," I said as my parents settled into the car and buckled their lap belts. "She lost her mother and her husband at the same time."

"Why did you think that it wasn't Thad?" Mom asked as Dad drove us home.

"It was that third coffee," I said, and leaned back and closed my eyes.

Chapter 23

"You couldn't let go of the idea that Vidalia bought a third coffee," Detective Murphy said from behind his desk.

I sat in one of the two plastic chairs facing him. Gage and Toby both waited for me in the front reception area.

The EMT had been right. I discovered a great deal of bruising all over my body. The worst part was my black eyes and the telltale finger bruises on my forearms. They were further proof of Anton's desperation. Detective Murphy had called this morning and asked me to come in and give an interview.

I had told him about the bruises and they had me go down to the Urgent Care Clinic where a female officer had shown up to record my injuries and my story. The urgent care doctor took X-rays of my right thumb, which had swollen up. It turns out it was only badly sprained. There were other unexpected bruises on my hands as well.

"Defensive wounds," the female officer whose name tag identified her as Officer Daye had said. "Solid proof that you are being honest with me."

"I am telling the truth," I said, upset by the idea that anyone would think I lied.

She smiled at me comfortingly. "Remember, everyone is innocent until proven guilty. These bruises substantiate your story. They will help provide a clear picture of what actually happened. It has nothing to do with your character."

Being a redhead, I was still insulted.

"Pepper?" Detective Murphy drew my attention back into the room. "Are you okay?"

"I'm fine." I fiddled with the sleeves of the sweater I had worn to cover the bruises. "What were you asking?"

His intelligent gaze went to my arms. "The bruises are a good thing, you know that, right? They show how much force he used when he kidnapped you."

I took a deep breath and blew it out slowly. "That's what Officer Daye said. Why am I so insulted?"

He smiled gently and leaned his elbows on his desk. "You are so much like my daughter. She, too, would bristle whenever I explained that evidence to back up your story is always best. It's not a matter of trusting your integrity, Pepper. This is helping to give us a preponderance of proof. It's what we need to go to trial and put Anton away."

"Did he confess to killing Eva?"

"He lawyered up," Detective Murphy said, his mouth creating a flat line.

"I wish I had recorded what he said on my phone. I didn't think of it."

"Of course, you didn't," he said. "You were fighting for your life. Now, tell me again how you knew it was Anton who killed Eva."

"It was the coffee," I said. "Something didn't feel right about the fact that Eva was killed when Vidalia went to the coffee shop. Whoever killed Eva had to know that she was alone in the shop. Anyone going in through the front risked being seen. So I went to see how easy it was to get to the shop from the alley. Then when Anton stepped out into the alley from the back of his shop, I realized that he could come and go unseen. Literally he could leave his work and go to Vidalia's shop and be back again without anyone knowing."

"Did you tell him that you knew he was the killer?"

I sat back and chewed on my bottom lip. "I might have, I can't remember. He came out asking me what I was looking for and I saw the fear in his eyes. Then I put it all together. I might have said something, but I think he knew I had figured it out from the look on my face. Being a redhead, every emotion shows. There's no hiding how I feel."

Detective Murphy nodded. "What happened then?"

"He grabbed me and pulled me into his shop. He sat me in a chair and explained to me that he could not let me ruin his family."

"Don't feel guilty about that," Detective Murphy said as his perceptive gaze studied me. "Anton is the one who ruined his family. What did he tell you?"

"He told me that Eva was going to change her will to include Vladimir. Anton believed that Vlad would crush the business Vidalia and Eva had worked so hard to build. He had asked Vidalia to set up a meeting with him and her mother so that they could all three sit together and hash out their concerns. That's why Vidalia bought three coffees."

"But he didn't wait for them to sit down, did he?"

"No." I shook my head and clasped my hands together in my lap. "He thought if he scared Eva, she would understand how important it was to Vidalia to keep the shop."

"That's crazy," Detective Murphy said.

"I know, right? Who thinks that threatening someone with a knife will ensure they do what you want? I mean, seriously, what did he expect to happen once he threatened her?" I frowned. "If a man threatened my mom, she would not only fight back like Eva, but she would tell me right away and I would call the cops on the guy. It wouldn't matter if we were married or not."

"He told you he went over to Bridal Dreams to threaten Eva into doing what he wanted?"

"Yes," I said. "He said things got out of hand. They struggled and Eva ended up dead. He didn't mean to kill her."

"Right, just threatened her with a knife," Detective Murphy said, and wrote something down. "Sick, that's what this guy is."

"Have you talked to Vidalia?" I asked.

"Yes, last night."

I drew my brows together. "What did she say?"

"She swore Anton would never hurt her mother. She still thinks he loved her mother."

"Did she know all along?" I said. "She brought him coffee."

"Vidalia believes that the killer killed her mother before Anton came over for the meeting," he said. "But we know otherwise." He sat back and his chair squeaked. "We interviewed Thad. He stated that he saw Anton in the alley right after he stole the goods. In fact, Thad was afraid that Anton would come after him, but instead Anton seemed focused on going into the back of the dress shop."

"You have an eyewitness," I said.

"We are collecting evidence," he said carefully. "Enough to take the case to the grand jury."

"Wow," I sat back. "Law is really complicated."

"It's not easy like you see on television. That said, I believe in the system. It's meant to keep everyone safe. It's why you need to leave solving murder cases to the professionals, Pepper."

I let my frown deepen. "I wasn't investigating . . . Okay, maybe I was, but only because that coffee bothered me. Vidalia had to have bought the coffee for the killer. I really doubt she bought it for Thad."

"We were working that angle, Pepper," Detective Murphy said softly.

"But you arrested Thad."

"We arrested him for the robbery and questioned him as a person of interest in Eva's murder," he corrected me. "It was my hope he would remember more of what happened that day if we got serious with him."

"Wait, it sounds as if Thad didn't suspect that Anton murdered Eva or he would have told you right away, wouldn't he? I mean, didn't he find it odd that Anton was in the alley?"

"Apparently Anton took the alley between shops all the time. Thad never put two and two together."

I sat back and frowned. "He doesn't seem like the brightest bulb in the bunch. It's why I never suspected that he did it." I looked at Detective Murphy. "What is Vidalia going to do now?"

"She said she was going to put the shop in both her and Vlad's name. It's what her mother truly wanted."

"And Anton?"

"Will be tried before a jury of his peers, unless he goes for a plea bargain."

I drew my brows together. "But he could say I was lying. Couldn't he?"

"We have him on kidnapping and assault charges," the detective said and leaned back in his chair to mirror me. "His lawyer will convince him to plead guilty and see if he can't get a lesser sentence."

Relief washed over me. Anton would not get out of jail for a while. Long enough for me to never go back to Bridal Dreams. The picture of Detective Murphy's daughter caught my eye. "How is your daughter doing? Is she still mad at you?"

He smiled and transformed his hound-dog face into one of pure joy. "She's coming for a weeklong visit for long games of Monopoly and hopefully some heart-to-heart talks. That's the plan anyway."

"It's a good plan," I said, as I gathered up my handbag and stood. "Thank you for telling me what is going on with Anton."

"You're welcome," he said, and pushed his chair up closer to his desk. "If he goes to trial, you'll be called as a witness."

"I know," I said with a small nod. "I can do it."

"Yes, you can, Pepper," he said. "You're a smart woman. Now go be with the men pacing outside in the waiting room."

"Thanks." I looked at my phone. "I've got to run. There's a proposal I'm planning in an hour."

"Take care, Pepper, and I mean that."

"Will do."

As I stepped into the waiting area, Gage and Toby stood. "Come on, my friends," I said. "We've got a proposal to see to."

Chapter 24

♂

The Music Box Theatre was packed with Mary and Joe's family and friends. The costumes were great. Several of the women wore hats that hid their faces. I had them sit closer to the couple's seats. Gage had brought some excellent props.

The huge plastic palm trees looked great next to the curtained screen. A baby grand piano sat in the orchestra pit, ready for the fake Humphrey Bogart to utter the classic line, "Play it again, Sam."

The costumes in the foyer were top flight. I had changed into a 1938 power suit of a mid-leg hemmed gray wool skirt with a matching gray wool blazer. The shoulder pads were crazy but suited my narrow-shouldered frame. The white cotton blouse that went with the outfit peeked out from the jacket. I wore seamed silk stockings, black high-heeled pumps, and killer red lipstick.

Gage gave a wolf whistle when he saw me. I blushed, heating my cheeks.

"You look swell," Gage said, and winked.

I did a little twirl. "They really knew how to cut clothes to create an hourglass figure."

"What do you think, Toby, my man?" Gage nudged Toby, winked, and made a figure eight shape in the air with his hands. "The broad is built."

Toby blushed as much as I did and stuck his finger between the stiff collar of his white dress shirt and his neck. "These collars are tight."

He and Gage both wore pinstriped suits from the time period with double-breasted coats and high-waisted wide-legged pants. "You both look fabulous," I said. Toby was less rumpled than usual but still looked not quite put together. I fixed a button he had missed on his jacket and patted him on the shoulder.

Gage's blue eyes crinkled. "Now, see, I should have left something unbuttoned."

"Why?"

He raised an eyebrow. "That way a gorgeous dame would stand real close and fix me." He winked.

I playfully smacked his arm. "You are incorrigible."

"Heads up," came the voice of my lookout up front.

"Places everyone," I said to the auditorium. Everyone faced forward and went silent. "Well, now, that's suspicious," I told the crowd. "Continue to talk as if you have no clue what is happening, but remember not to turn around or Joe might recognize you. Okay?"

"Okay!" said the crowd in unison.

I grabbed the Humphrey Bogart impersonator named Fred. "Come on, kid, you're on. Greet them at the door and encourage them to get into costume."

"Will do," Fred said.

I let him go to the lobby area as I headed back to check that the emcee was ready. Gage and Toby were stationed on either side of the stage to help with the details of the show where needed. Gage cut quite a figure in his suit, tall with broad shoulders and lean hips. Toby on the other hand was shorter and thicker, but still looked good.

I was surprised at how interested Toby seemed in the proposal business. I certainly hoped he finally understood what it took to ask someone to marry him and live happily ever after.

The emcee was Paul Douglas. He was dressed like an announcer from the late thirties, his hair slicked back and his plaid suit carefully understated. Well, as understated as plaid could be on a man. "Do you have the ring?"

"Right here." He patted his inside right breast pocket. "Got the lines memorized. It'll be great."

I sent him a thumbs-up and caught Cesar's eye. My videographer had even gotten into the act, wearing a full navy suit and pale blue shirt with a red bowtie. "Hey, Cesar, are you missing the entrance?"

"No, I set up cameras that cover everything from the ticket line to the costume racks and the doors. We'll catch every angle."

"Great."

"I'm going to head down to the entrance and catch them getting seated by Bogart. That way it looks like it's all part of the act."

"Perfect." I watched him go. I had instructed Mary to tell Joe that the theater was filming for a television commercial. It would explain the camera on Bogart and the emcee and the stage.

The lights dimmed. The doors opened and a spotlight popped up. Mary came in on Joe's arm. The spotlighted Bogart showed the way to their seats. Cesar played the part, pretending to shoot mostly the impersonator, but he was actually catching the couple.

The theater grew quiet as they found their seats. Bogart made his way down to the orchestra pit as the piano player started playing his song. The impersonator sat down next to the pianist on the piano seat, listened carefully, and then uttered the famous line.

The audience went wild and Cesar appeared to pan the crowd. "And go!" I said, cueing the emcee to step out.

"Good evening, ladies and gentlemen. Thank you for coming out to this evening's *Casablanca* extravaganza. Tonight's event includes not only a visit from Mr. Humphrey Bogart himself"—Paul paused and waved toward the impersonator and the crowd applauded—"but the complete movie with pre-censor scenes. We are showing the film on projector instead of digital recording so that you can view it in all its original glory. This means that we will have a short intermission while they change reels."

He walked to the center of the stage. "Never fear, during intermission we will have an interview with Mr. Bogart and take questions from the audience. But for now, sit back, relax, and . . . enjooooy the show." He did a full theater sweep with his arm and the spotlight went out, the curtains opened, and the show began.

The scent of popcorn filled the air. Concession girls walked up and down the aisle offering popcorn, candy, and drinks out of trays that hung around their necks. Joe bought popcorn and Cracker Jacks. The peanut and caramel corn confection included a prize inside. He and Mary shared a large soda with two straws. A cuter couple I had never seen.

Finally it was intermission time. As the lights went up, the emcee stepped out. "Ladies and gentlemen, before you leave your seats we have a very special event tonight. Oscar, the spotlight." He pointed at Mary and Joe. The spotlight went straight to my couple. I clasped my hands together, suddenly uncertain that this was going to play out in a good way.

"Would Mary Ketchum and Joe Jones come down to the stage," Paul said.

Mary pointed at herself, her hand grabbing Joe's for support.

"Yes, you, come on down," Paul said, and waved them down. "Come on, everyone, it appears they need a little encouragement." He started to clap and the entire audience clapped and hollered as the two made their way to the stage. Paul turned Mary and Joe toward the crowd. I knew they couldn't see the audience. I had tested the lighting myself. I saw Joe shade his eyes as he tried to peer out. Paul was quick to turn him away from the audience. "Joe, would you please have a seat, right here." He steered Joe to a simple chair that the stagehands had brought out. Joe sat, facing the side of the stage.

"Now, Mary," Paul said, and pulled Mary into place in front of Joe. "I understand that you and Joe have been dating a few years, is that right?"

"Yes," Mary said, her hands trembling. "We've been dating for three years."

"And you like movies?"

"We both like movies," Mary said and looked at Joe. "Black-and-white movies. In fact *Casablanca* is Joe's favorite."

"Really?" Paul turned to Joe. "Can you do the quote?" He put the microphone in front of Joe.

"Of all the gin joints in all the world, she had to walk into mine," Joe said into the mic and laughed.

"Can you do it with the accent?" The mic went from Paul back to Joe.

Game for a try, Joe said it again in his best Bogart imitation.

"Now that calls for applause, don't you think everyone?" Paul waved his free hand and had the audience cheering. Then he turned to Mary and took a small box out of his pocket. "Mary, I think there was a question you wanted to ask Joe, wasn't there?"

"Yes," Mary said, and took the box, and then she faced Joe and got down on one knee. "I know this is a little unexpected, but there comes a time in a girl's life when she just knows what she wants. Joe, I want you. Will you marry me?" She opened the box to show a silver band with a Celtic knot.

Joe shook his head.

My heart froze for a moment and I held my breath.

Then he grinned. "Yes, of course."

The entire audience broke out in cheers as Joe stood and pulled Mary to her feet and hugged her tight, then whirled her round until her feet swung out. My eyes filled with tears and I covered my mouth with my clasped hands.

Joe stopped and grabbed the microphone. "I want you all to know that I was going to ask Mary the same question tonight." He held up the Cracker Jack box and pulled the prize out of the box. In his hand was a sparkling diamond.

The cheers from the audience raised the roof as Mary stood there crying happy tears. Joe turned and put his ring on Mary's left finger and Mary put her ring on his. "Well, there you go, folks. Now that is a sight worth waiting for, isn't it?"

The happy couple kissed. Paul pulled the curtain around them to give them some privacy. The audience was still on its feet cheering. He had to wave them down so that he could speak.

"Ladies and gentlemen, please take fifteen minutes and when we come back we'll interview Mr. Bogart and finish the show. Afterwards, please follow the ushers to the second floor where an engagement banquet awaits."

The house lights went up and the audience rushed the stage. Mary and Joe were pulled out from behind the curtain for hugs and kisses.

"Perfect," I said, and looked at Gage on the other side of the curtain. He sent me a big thumbs-up. I smiled and put my thumbs up in response.

"I think I get it," Toby said beside me.

"You do?" I asked, my voice and eyebrows rising.

"Yes," he said. "It's that look in their eyes as if they have just been handed the moon and all their dreams have come true."

"Exactly," I said, and patted his padded shoulder.

"It's the same look you have when you look at Gage," he said, his hound-dog expression slightly sad.

"Wait, what?" I shook my head, confused.

"That look the couple has, you have it whenever you look at him." Toby nodded his head toward Gage.

"Oh," I said, and the heat of a blush rushed up my neck and over my ears. "Oh, no, we just sort of started dating." I glanced at Gage, who watched to ensure the crowd didn't trample his palm trees.

"Say what you will." Toby shrugged and shoved his hands in his pockets. "The eyes don't lie."

"I'm sure I got caught up in the moment, that's all," I said. "Excuse me. I need to make sure that the engagement party will be ready to go by the end of the movie. I'm glad you finally get it, Toby. Stay if you want. The food is from Morelli's. It's really good, plus there's an open bar."

"Don't worry," he said, his gaze suddenly less sad. "I've decided to stick around a while."

Chapter 25

"I'm so sorry to hear about your husband, Vidalia," Felicity said as she stood in her wedding gown. It was the second fitting. The one where Felicity wore her shoes and undergarments so that they could hem the dress and finalize the alterations.

"It is terrible," Vidalia said with her mouth full of pins as she held them in between her teeth before she placed them on the hem. "I still cannot believe it. Anton was a good man." She shook her head. "But now, I must divorce him, of course, and start over."

"Yes. But you'll be okay. I am certain of that," I said from my perch on the stage beside Felicity's riser. I was in my maid of honor gown with Theresa on her knees pinning my hem as quickly as Vidalia pinned my sister's.

"What a terrible thing he did, all because he didn't want your brother, Vlad, to be part of your shop."

"At least I am not alone. Theresa and I are both single now, right Theresa?" Vidalia said.

"Yes," Theresa said and nodded vehemently as she pinned. "When I found out that Thad had stolen those gowns, I dumped him right away. I am so lucky that Vidalia let me keep my job after what he did."

"Well, we are in similar situations, yes?" Vidalia said. "I could not fire you for something a man did."

"Wow, that is so wise of you," I said to Vidalia. "Others might not have given Theresa the same chance."

"She knows if she sees him again she is fired," Vidalia stated.

"Oh, I won't see him," Theresa said. "I have learned my lesson."

"As have I," Vidalia agreed.

"Speaking of men in the shop, was that Vlad out in the reception area?" my mother asked from her riser where she stood wearing her mother-of-the-bride outfit.

Vidalia had picked out a beautiful silk shantung suit for my mother. The cut fit her figure and the color flattered her coloring. All together we looked pretty good, if I had to say so myself. Felicity glowed and Mom's and my outfits complemented her perfectly. Cesar was going to be able to get some great shots for this wedding, which was still three months away.

"Yes, that is my brother, Vlad," Vidalia said as she pulled the pins from her mouth and quickly navigated the yards of fabric on the gown and train. "I have had my lawyers work a new agreement where my brother owns half of the shop. I have vowed to rebuild both the dress shop and my family."

"Well, this certainly is a good start," my mother said and motioned with her hand toward Felicity and I.

"Yes, yes," Vidalia nodded her agreement. "Thanks to the Pomeroy family for not only solving my mother's murder, but for returning to my shop. The promotion materials you have sent out at your engagement parties—"

"Perfect Proposals," I corrected her.

"Yes, proposals," she said. "They have filled my entire datebook. I will need Vlad to work reception and perhaps get a second girl. I have so many requests now."

"Good," my mother said.

"It's all in a day's work," I said, and smiled at my own reflection. I, too, had gotten five appointments out of the last two engagements I had thrown. It seems that I had found my perfect life. Well, perfect might be a bit of an exaggeration, but I certainly was more happy, healthy, and free than I had been in years. And that made the future look very bright. Very bright indeed.

Skydiving Engagement Party Menu

BASED ON THE MENU FROM PAN AM'S INAUGURAL FLIGHT
FROM THE UNITED STATES TO NEW ZEALAND ON SEPTEMBER
11, 1940.

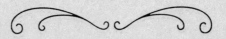

First Course

OPEN WITH GIN AND VODKA MARTINIS
OR MANHATTANS AND FRESH HORS D'OEUVRES
MADE OF CHILLED UTAH CELERY; GREEN,
RIPE STAFFORD OLIVES; ASSORTED NUTS;
AND GARDEN RADISHES

Second Course

GRAPEFRUIT MARASCHINO
(BAKED GRAPEFRUIT WITH MARASCHINO
CHERRIES) / CONSUME MADRILENE
(MADE WITH TOMATOES, BELL PEPPERS, LEEKS,
EGG WHITES, AND CHICKEN STOCK)

Third Course

GRILLED FILET MIGNON AU BEURRE /
SHOESTRING POTATOES / FRESH GARDEN PEAS

Fourth Course

CHEF SALAD WITH FRENCH DRESSING

Fifth Course

INDIVIDUAL ICE CREAMS—CHOCOLATE,
STRAWBERRY, VANILLA / DUCHESS CAKE—
CHIFFON CAKE WITH RASPBERRY FILLING
AND WHIPPED CREAM FROSTING

Sixth Course

AMERICAN, SWISS, AND EDAM CHEESE / SALTINES
AND RITZ WAFERS / COFFEE, TEA, AND MILK

Seventh Course

ASSORTED FRESH FRUITS

Finale

AFTER DINNER MINTS